WELCOME to one of the CEMETERIES in AMERICA!

BACHELORS GROVE CEMETERY, where LEGEND and LIES meet …

In the first part of this book, you'll learn what goes into a horror comic script and one man's journey to become a published scripter in the independent comics field.

In addition to FOUR annotated comic scripts for *The Haunting Tales of Bachelors Grove* comic, there are FOUR horror prose stories, THREE of which have been written JUST for this book.

Ghostly Madonnas, retreating farm houses, demonic possession, haunted highways, and a footrace for life itself.

No costumed crusaders.

No super powers.

No classic novels played for laughs.

Come visit the dark side of Brian K. Morris

The Haunting Scripts of Bachelors Grove

by

Brian K. Morris

Inspired by the Silver Phoenix Entertainment
Comic Book Anthology

The Haunting Tales

of

Bachelors Grove

Created by **Charles D. Moisant**

Published by

Rising Tide Publications

A Division of

Freelance Words

In cooperation with

Silver Phoenix Entertainment

3

Editor: **Cookie Morris**

Art Director: **Trevor Erick Hawkins**

Cover Illustrator: **Trevor Erick Hawkins**

Rising Tide Logo Designer: **Eric Hawkins**

Editorial Consultant: **Charles D. Moisant**

ISBN# 978-0-9993082-0-2

First RISING TIDE Printing: February 2018

Contents

Introduction

by
Charles D. Moisant

(This essay was transcribed from a recording found on Charles D. Moisant's phone four nights ago.)

The name, "Bachelors Grove," it just seemed so strange, interesting, and lonely.

When I was in high school, I had a good friend, Johnny – I won't say his last name, but he was into the "arts," we'll just say – and we would go and investigate this strange and forbidden area. It was dilapidated, graves sunk in, things like that. A myriad of ghost stories was talked about, Satanic cults supposedly around, murders, and things just rich with stories.

Obviously, there were stories about drunken teenagers, debauchery, and all this other fun stuff. When you're sixteen, seventeen, fifteen, fourteen, the place was creepy and kind of exciting.

We tried to look for proof of entities haunting the cemetery. What I really found interesting about the place was that if you saw the House, and you walked towards it, it receded. But if it didn't, and you entered it, you might disappear. For the Pond, it was recorded that lots of mobsters were dropped into it, so who knows what type of dark entities lie in there?

Then, of course, the stories about the Fulton grave pulling things in, of being this dark overlord over the cemetery. And then had the gravestone that says "INFANT" on it. Sometimes, gravestones would just be found in the middle of the Pond. How did they get there? They were far too heavy for even four or five strong men to pick up. They'd have to use a machine. It was just very curious.

One of my friends found human femurs leading into a trail that led nowhere. He actually contacted the police on that and the strange thing about the femurs was that they were actually from female bones from the 1800's. That was weird!

Myself, I slipped and fell. I hit the ground and I started to sink into the ground, into a rotted-out coffin. Moments later, my back started itching and when I got up, my friend told me there were thousands of grave mosquitoes covering my back. And with all that ichor and gross stuff, hours later, my back looked like the worst case of acne a person could ever experience.

Fortunately, I didn't get malaria or anything devastating, but my back was badly, badly infected ... kinda neat, in a way, too, because I could now say I had proof I'd been "kissed" by the Bachelors Grove.

Early in college, I tried to write a story called "A Haunted Story," about a young man who befriended a vampire. I was trying to say monsters aren't aberrants. Sometimes, they could do good deeds, even though the long-term goal was something nefarious. I loosely based it on Bachelors Grove, where a vampire wanted to seduce and totally enthrall a young person to become a devotee, very similar to the Swedish vampire film, *Let the Right One In*.

But time went on and I never really moved forward with the story, so it went to the back burner.

Many years later, I got out of publishing comic books because of my financial crashes, the death of my brother, and a few other events that happened, but that story was always in the back of my mind. A part of me thought, "Where do I go from there?"

I was then reminded that the anthology story format could really work for Bachelors Grove. In fact, what if I did something different and really worked with the myths, that the House was a living entity, just dark and horrific? And the Cemetery was evil. It just wanted to be left alone Also, the

Pond was hungry and vicious? And instead of having storytellers like traditional anthology stories, the entities of Bachelors Grove told the story.

I thought how much fun this would be.

I came up with a concept for a vampire, to really make it something viable, vile, horrible, horrific, disgusting, awful. What would really unnerve someone when it came to a vampire? Have the soul tethered, watching their body commit atrocities. I'd never seen that done.

It's interesting because a lot of people look at this and say, "Wow! This is kinda cool." Except for those who are very religious. They find it horrifying.

I wanted the books to have some of the best artwork I've ever produced for comics. I initially bounced some ideas off Michael Reidy and we came up with a partial concept for a story with a haunted house. But it fell to the back burner too ...

... until I met Brian K. Morris. He is a VORACIOUS writer. For him, basically, it's an addiction, the best type of addiction because something good comes from it. He will write this, write that, write this, write that, and after a while, we just started developing things together and stories just were flowing. It was amazing! Incredible! We had almost found each other as MUSES and motivation.

It was like we couldn't fail!

Well, Brian referred some artists, I had some, Mike Reidy still wanted to do his story, but he wanted to take it over completely, which was fine. I came up with some concepts, Brian wrote a lot of scripts, edited a lot more from some newly-recruited writers, and BOOM! That worked for the first book. Not only that, but we picked up a couple of live people who wanted to be written into the universe of Bachelors Grove.

Ron Fitzgerald was the first, a local illusionist and Master of the Dark Arts, and gross, dark, sticky fun. We decided to make him a major character. We also reached out to Kadrolsha Ona and she jumped at the chance to be incorporated into the comic universe. She was very happy, and both were very excited when they saw our plans.

Then we did a Kickstarter and it went really well.

Getting out the first issue was a little rocky. A lot of personal things got in the way, and it took a while, so for that, I apologize. But person after person after person who received the book all said it was worth the wait. It's been very, very exciting.

Now, the reaction I'm getting from the public, from reviews, have been awe-inspiring phenomenal. The only other time I'd gotten something as good was with my Bane of the Werewolf, which was one of my top comics at the time. Sadly, that only one issue was able to be produced and I thought that was the highlight of what I could do as comics.

I finally matched, if not exceeded it. I'll exceed it when more books are out. So, spread the word.

I think the reason this book did so well was just the appeal of what horror really is ... something to be feared and when you're done with the reading, you're grateful that it's not you.

I just love this medium and I guess my addition's producing comics. I've gotta make comics, I've gotta make stories. I'd love to do animation and films and who knows? Maybe things will happen from this to allow that.

Wait a second. I hear something scratching at the door. I ...

(The Midlothian Police Department revealed in a press conference that Charles D. Moisant's vehicle was located across the street from Bachelors Grove Cemetery. There were clear signs of a one-sided struggle and Moisant's body was nowhere to be found.)

(UPDATE, THREE DAYS LATER: A police spokesperson claimed that the phone belonging to Charles D. Moisant had gone missing from the Evidence lock-up. Security cameras picked up no one and an internal investigation was underway.)

(UPDATE, LAST NIGHT: In a new e-mail from Charles D. Moisant to Brian K. Morris: "Ask no questions. I have an idea for a new vampire story. Meet me at B.G. to discuss. Come alone. Tell no one.")

Spoiler Warnings Abound

This book contains scripts that have not, as of this printing, been assigned to illustrators as well as information that might reveal the endings of some stories yet to be printed.

You also might have every intention of purchasing every issue of *The Haunting Tales of Bachelors Grove* – and God bless you if this is the case – but haven't mastered the necessary time management skills, nor the funding to make this a reality. In which case, the stories may be published, but you might not have seen them yet.

So, you enter this book with the full knowledge that I will potentially, and negatively, affect your reading experience when you finally pick up *The Haunting Tales of Bachelors Grove*, which you should. You really should.

From this point on, you're on your own. Have fun anyway.

Special Notes and Acknowledgements

The scripts in this book will be the final edited ones prior to assignment to an artist. In some cases, for various unforeseen reasons, the scripts required rewriting just prior to publication and what you see here may differ from the final, printed version. However, we present them in their approved forms in the interest of education and history.

Special thanks to my beta reading army: **Amy Hale, Amy Schwartze, Angie Meloy, Candice Gilligan, Charlie Cargile, Donald York, Emily Yates, Gary Buettner, Jackie McCord, Jamie Beals, Jason Nugent, Jim Bosomworth, Katie Peterson, Kenneth Huff, Mark Learnard, Nathaniel Sims, Pamela Rachiell, Pauly Hart, Rick Welchans, Sage Stafford, Sam Campbell, Steve Chaney**, and **Teresa Dunn**. You are my heroes!

Many thanks to **Jennifer Hewett**, the Managing Editor at *Georgia Magazine*, as always. Check out her work at www.georgiamagazine.com.

And a personal thank you to everyone who supported the Kickstarter campaign for *The Haunting Tales of Bachelors Grove* #1. I also thank you for your patience in my getting this publication out.

This book is dedicated to **CHARLES D. MOISANT** who brought me into his world of madness and love. Thank you for being my friend!

Chapter One - The Cemetery Dies & Is Reborn

Who would think that a cemetery could die? Or come back to life once again?

The area that would become Midlothian, Illinois, from what records survive from that time, was well-populated by the time four different men

What truly became Bachelors Grove Cemetery began life, so to speak, around 1864 when Edward D Everdon sold a sizeable parcel of land to Frederick Schmidt who designated one acre to be used as a cemetery. Although plans may have existed to expand the graveyard as needed, the cemetery never sold enough plots to warrant it.

However, the traffic patterns changed, and the cemetery was used less and less. Out of sight, out of mind, as it were. Plans to create an entrance on 143rd Street to the grounds failed to gain the necessary clearances through the woods that surrounded the property. Sometime in the 1960s, the road leading up to the front gate of Bachelors Grove Cemetery was closed to vehicular traffic.

By this time, what used to be a showplace where families once went to picnic on Sundays while visiting their loved ones, now became a hangout for teenagers to make out. Soon, vandals entered the isolated cemetery, destroying, and sometimes stealing the grave markers as well as some bodies. Police found evidence of Satanic rituals being held there.

The last internment at Bachelors Grove occurred in 1989. The previous burial on those grounds happened 24 years earlier.

Stories circulated about many paranormal events occurring at Bachelors Grove. Voices rode the winds, tortured and crying out to loved ones, long since passed. An ectoplasmic farmhouse receded from view as you approached it. Specific areas of the grounds neutralized electronic equipment from phones to electromagnetic measuring devices. Racing blue and red lights pursued unwary visitors as did phantoms and even automobiles. An ax-wielding caretaker safeguarded the cemetery from intruders while a ghostly Madonna appeared in photographs as she gazed into a realm invisible to mortal eyes.

In fact, a legend circulated that Al Capone once dumped his enemies' bodies in the pond that lay on the north side of the cemetery. No known attempt has ever been made to verify or disprove this claim.

Now, Midlothian Boulevard is a wide path through a dense, intimidating forest with strips of asphalt to give evidence that a road had ever been there. In fact, the path is virtually invisible from 143rd Street due to overgrowth as well as a large concrete building that belongs to the power company.

To reach the cemetery, one must park across the street at a forest preserve. After crossing four lanes of traffic, not including a turn lane, you walk behind the concrete building, with many thick electrical cables leading into it, over an uneven patch of gravel, then onto the road that quite a distance later, leads the traveler to the cemetery's entrance.

The easiest way to enter the cemetery today is on foot. Once you pass the sign that states the illegality of your presence inside the grounds after sunset, the outside world closes off to your senses. Unshielded, vulnerable, you walk along the former road where infrequent strips of asphalt remain as evidence that automobiles once traveled this path.

As you walk, the twisted trees seize your attention and you wonder what might live beyond the relative safety of the road. Even the most cynical of disbelievers in the paranormal might feel a presence – no, presences surrounding you, observing you, judging you.

Only a handful of gravestones remain to commemorate the bodies still there ... assuming they weren't stolen, or the families had the caskets exhumed and transferred to another cemetery. A wire fence surrounds the cemetery grounds while another prevents easy access to the pond. Through small gaps in the unfettered greenery, one can see traffic moving along 143rd Street. However, the sound of their travel barely penetrates the eerie silence of the Grove.

Time, weather, and vandalism have worn away many of the grave markers. One large stone dominates the Grove and as you walk around it, your breath frozen in your lungs, you gasp as you see the children's toys laid decoratively around a headstone with no name.

You cannot recall a time when you *wanted* to see Bachelors Grove. Now, you cannot wait to escape, to rejoin the safety of the mundane world. Such is the power of Bachelors Grove Cemetery.

Through condemnation and examination of the heirs of Edward Everdon, The Cemetery Trustees of the Cook County Board assumed responsibility for what remains of Bachelors Grove Cemetery circa 1976. Today, the Board shares maintenance responsibility with the Cook County Forest Preserve District.

Even with the various intergovernmental agreements concerning Bachelors Grove, the cemetery grounds had become overgrown. However, a local group of volunteers, The Grove Restoration Project, has assisted with maintaining the property, to increase positive awareness of the cemetery and his history, as well as maintaining a website, **www.bachelorsgrove.com** that's well worth checking out.

Chapter Two - Enter "The Craziest Man in Comics"

In the early 1980s, it was possible to buy one copy of virtually every comic book available with the average American paycheck. By the early '90s, not even comic shops could afford a copy of everything because of the sheer number of new publishers entering the field.

So, what was one more?

Charles D. Moisant released his first comic title in 1991 under the Grey Entertainment imprint. *Kremin* was a high-concept series about a trans-phase dimensional-hopping adventurer. The first issue, written and drawn by Charles, sold over 4,000 copies, making it a success.

Unfortunately, an error in the Diamond *Previews* catalog, using another comic's description in error, killed *Kremin*'s sales by over 75%. Then Charles' brother passed away, forcing Charles to use Gray Entertainment's publishing money to pay for the funeral. By issue four, *Kremin* and Gray Entertainment were no more.

During a 2005 road trip through Omaha, Charles and his friend, Sean Sullivan, stopped at Wayne Sealey's Mystery Manor, a "haunted" amusement house. While working there in October, Charles created the persona of Dr. Wayne Zarvin, a well-meaning scientist wracked with the guilt of his failures. Sealey and Charles discussed the possibility of turning the Mystery Manor concept into a comic book. All Charles needed would be a publisher.

Fortunately for the duo, in 2006, Elizabeth J. Moisant launched Silver Phoenix Entertainment, Inc., naming her son Charles as the Creative Director of Silver Phoenix Entertainment. This gave Charles the vehicle to publish six issues of *Wayne Seeley's Mystery Manor*, the first issue of which sold over 20,000 copies.

In 2008, Elizabeth and Charles fell for a Ponzi scheme, losing over $110,000 in the process. The Moisants helped the FBI capture the perpetrator of the scheme, but their publishing empire, as well as their personal finances, took a sizeable hit from which they've still not recovered.

Despite not having deep publishing pockets, Charles continued to publish his unique brand of high concept comic books, often just one a year when finances allowed. Charles also strove to overcome a debilitating case of dyslexia, which limited his writing output.

The titles from Silver Phoenix included *Whispers From the Void* (monstrosities based on The Seven Deadly Sins), *Wayne Sealey's Haunted Mansion* (a horror anthology based on a real-life haunted house exhibit), *Roller Derby Drama* (skating grrls with super powers), *Blood Feast* (a tale of cannibalism sponsored by a local German restaurant), *Zombie Apocalypse* (a salute to the B-Movie Sci-Fi films of Charles' youth, drawn in a style that salutes the genius of Jack Kirby), a 2014 non-fiction history of Oak Park, Illinois, and *Myth Tales* (based on the Robert Asprin-created series of books, scripted by current chronicler, fantasy writer Jody Lynn Nye).

Despite his limited resources, Charles attracted some name talent from DC, Marvel, Wildstorm, and many independent companies to work for Silver Phoenix. While the releases were infrequent, Charles' innovations made them worth waiting for. And no one was more enthusiastic about the company's output than Charles himself.

Ever seeking new territory to explore, Charles recalled visits to a local cemetery in his younger, somewhat wilder years. On one journey, he discovered many century-old human bones sticking out of the soil. On another, he literally fell into an old grave and developed a rash that left his doctor puzzled, almost as if hundreds of red ants bit his back at once.

That cemetery, of course, was Bachelors Grove.

Chapter Three - Recruiting & The Background

Charles researched the history of Bachelors Grove Cemetery, becoming more excited by the story possibilities. He also added his own spin on the classic vampire legend. Instead of infecting their prey with whatever brand of cooties that transformed normal humans into blood-drinking, bat-becoming, sunlight-avoiding parasites, these vampires became free-roaming demons who possessed their human shells and imbued them with other-worldly powers.

However, the souls of the original occupants were tethered to their former bodies by their chakras, forced to witness the atrocities committed. Some would go mad, some would become corrupted, others would find the strength to resist. But if that psychic tether was ever broken, the soul would die.

This version of Bachelors Grove came with some ground rules that would lift it above the standard Shelley or Stoker-influenced horror story. Although Charles quantified his concepts in terms of Dungeons & Dragons statistics, he invented different "personalities" for the triumvirate that made up the burial grounds.

The Pond, female in nature, where Al Capone allegedly

dumped the bodies of some of his enemies, was constantly ravenous. It could expand to overflowing when needed. It also housed various nefarious beings yet to be discovered.

On the other hand, the Cemetery was filled to bursting and wanted no more bodies inside her. She felt like a pregnant human female whose due date had come and gone long ago.

Then there was a Farmhouse that receded from view as you approached it. Being the male component of the trio, its job was to judge anyone who managed to cross his threshold. It could also teleport and become any sort of building it wished.

In addition, there was a spectral groundsman and a ghostly Madonna who wandered the cemetery in silence. There were also zombies, the aforementioned vampires, and many other deviants, with the exception of werewolves.

Once the foundation was laid for his stories, all that remained to do would be to find some creators to work on the stories, many of which Charles would provide.

However, to chronicle that process, this narrative needs to switch from first to third-person, four paragraphs from now.

Chapter Four - The First Scripts

In recent years, Charles became a frequent guest at conventions, often with his good friend, former Disney/Hanna-Barbera/Don Bluth/Filmation animator Philo Barnhart. As Philo sketched and regaled visitors with tales from his Hollywood upbringing, Charles roller skated from one end of the venue to the other, wearing his tie-dyed lab coat.

And when not selling Philo's many art prints, Charles hawked his own.

In 2015, at Nerd Con in Robinson, Illinois, Charles set up his wares in one corner of the auditorium and began his usual carny barker yelling as he moved from one end of the hall to the other. Smiling as he drew the attendees' attention towards his table, he heard a voice, one as loud and as cheerful as his own:

"Cheer the hell up, willya?"

Now comes the awkward switch to first-person narrative.

As Nerd Con wound down, I walked over to the man I'd been heckling for most of the afternoon. We began talking and he noticed that I wrote a LOT of stuff. At that time, I had *Santastein: The Post-Holiday Prometheus, Conflict: A Study in Heroic Contrasts*, and *Vulcana: Rebirth of the Champion* for sale on my table.

I guess the quirky nature of the books amused Charles enough to describe the Bachelors Grove universe to me. I was intrigued, especially since I wanted to add more comic book work to my resume, having done an issue of *Celebration Comics* from BiMor Comics and had placed a script with another small publisher.

Charles was probably happy with my background in writing, from stage plays to advertising to mini-comics to novels and short stories. I liked the idea that the stories would not be bathed in gore, nudity, and excessive swearing. To me, that kind of "shock value" was far too easy, having no shock and certainly little value. My own influences were the character-driven classic EC Comics such as *Tales From the Crypt* and *The Vault of Horror*, along with DC Comics' *The House of Mystery, Tales of the Unexpected, The Witching Hour, Ghosts*, and *The House of Secrets* and the monster/sci-fi comics of the years prior to the Marvel Age of Comics.

In addition, the good guys would survive these stories. Yeah, they might have major PTSD issues, but at least they'd be alive. By contrast, anyone who crossed any moral boundaries would get their comeuppance and how!

We parted that night, promising to talk more.

Coincidentally, both Charles and I were both booked the next day as guests at Chris McQuillan's ToyMan Toy & Comic Show in Bridgeton, MO. After talking more that day, we decided to work together on this project. I'd write, and he'd edit with the help of his mother, publisher Elizabeth Moisant.

And that proved to be just the start …

Chapter Five - Dark, Sticky Goth Fun & The Queen of the Paranormal

I began working on some scripts in due order. My first script was a tale entitled "A Loser's Race," concerning the Farmhouse and one unfortunate lad who managed to catch it. This story was spun strictly from my imagination and my second attempt to write comic book horror, the first being a story in *Celebration Comics* #2, featuring The Purple Claw (BiMor Comics, edited by Sean Dulaney, 2016).

As Charles traveled across The Fruited Plains, he encountered other writers and attempted to bring them into the fold. Many of them came from the realms of screenplays, novels, and other comics. A few of them, I still don't know why he recruited them, aside from possessing a pulse. But enough of that particular rant.

While my scripts began to drop into Charles' e-mailbox, I started seeing scripts from other writers entering my own account. I asked why …

Charles: "You're now my editor on *The Haunting Tales of Bachelors Grove*."

Me: "Oh, okay."

Charles liked how I could dissect a script and articulate

exactly why I did or didn't enjoy a specific aspect of the script. I guess that's how I got the gig.

Soon, I'm reading scripts, accepting a few, asking for rewrites on others, and kneading fresh talents into thinking within the limited confines of the comics page. Some dropped out along the way when they realized 1) that like other forms of writing, the editor will ask for rewrites, and 2) writing comics is freakin' HARD! When one must boil down a story into six or fewer pages, six or fewer panels per page, and 35 words per panel with a cumulative total of 200 words, or fewer, on each page (with an allowance for the extra space that sound effects take up). But the ones who stuck around came up with some thrilling results.

And the few scripts I rejected came from people who just didn't get the format. One problem with many writers for the small presses, both in prose as well as comic books, is that too many want-to-be-in-print creators don't check into a company's output or simply figure we indie publishers will accept anything because we're awesome like that.

Fact is that even though Silver Phoenix was still a small fry operation, Charles and I still had big fry standards. I rejected story ideas from people who wanted to write superhero stories along with other genres that Silver Phoenix didn't publish, writers who only did prose and expected Charles or myself to adapt their work for comics (when my workload lightened or Hell froze over, whichever came last) or just didn't understand the unique limitations of the comic scripting form, as well as one guy who always showed up at a certain convention every year to pitch his 30-year old books concerning the care and operation of the Vic 20 home computer. Um, thanks but no thanks.

So how did one break into comics? In times past, one prepared a script on speculation and submitted it to an editor at a specific company. However, due to the huge number of people wanting to enter the field, many comic book publishers stopped reading those scripts. In fact, they ceased considering unsolicited manuscripts altogether. In other words, you didn't call them, they'd call you ... um, no, they wouldn't.

Today, unless you have an agent, a contact at a company, or sufficiently impressive credits, there's no sense in prepping a script for the big companies. In fact, some writers start out as an editorial assistant or in some other area of comic book production. For instance, Peter David moved from a sales position at Marvel Comics to become one of their top-flight scripters. Prolific writer Bill Mantlo was once a colorist, Chris Claremont was a summer intern for Marvel Comics, and Steve Engelhart entered the industry as an artist.

So how does someone build a resume for comic book writing? First of all, write scripts. Get the sucky ones out of your system and keep working at your craft. Approach writing the way Michael Jordan worked towards becoming one of the greatest basketball players of all time. He shot baskets every day, thousands and thousands of times, until he was good enough to join the NBA.

So, write, write, write. Also, read as much as you can. Study the styles of your favorite writers so you'll know what to emulate in your style. Also look at those stories you don't enjoy, avoiding those aspects of writing in your own style.

Listen to all criticism and pick out the information that will help you grow as a creator. Ignore everything else so your ego become bulletproof. Network with other creators and seek out the smaller companies who might print your work. Or else go online and soak up the information on YouTube or the search engine of your choice on what it would take to publish your own work.

And be patient. There is no such thing as an "overnight success." Enjoy the journey.

There are also many great books on writing that you can probably order through your local library. I personally recommend *On Writing* by Stephen King, *Telling Lies for*

Fun and Profit by Lawrence Block, *The DC Guide To Writing Comics* by Dennis J. O'Neil, *Stan Lee's How To Write Comics* by Stan Lee with Robert Greenberger, and the exceptional book, *Write or Wrong* by Dirk Manning.

But anyway, about Bachelors Grove ...

During this time, I also tagged along with Charles and Philo to sell my wares, as well as those of Silver Phoenix. Soon, I was asked to give my opinions of art samples from potential contributors and Charles continually asked me whose illustrative skills would be appropriate for which story.

Me: "Charles, why are you asking me about the art?"

Charles: "Because you're my Editor-in-chief for the entire Silver Phoenix line."

Me: "Oh, okay."

As we toured, together or separately, the buzz built for not only our *Bachelors Grove* comic, but another upcoming book entitled *The History of the Police in America.* I quickly told people that no, it wasn't about Andy, Stewart, and Sting on the *Synchronicity* tour. It was a recounting of the history of uniformed law enforcement as told through the eyes of a multi-cultural family.

(*THOTPIA*, with art by Jeffrey Moy and a script by me, is intended as an outreach tool for every police department in America. You'll be hearing more about this, trust me.)

At CIL-Con, a paranormal convention in Mattoon, Illinois, Charles and I set up there, him for Silver Phoenix and me for my own publishing work. Charles ran up to me on the second day ...

Charles: "I just got Ron Fitzgerald to be in our book and you're going to be the writer."

Me: "Oh, okay."

Master Ron Fitzgerald was a Chicago-based illusionist as well as an MC and very talented actor. I introduced myself to Ron and he told me about his act that would go on in a couple of hours. Wanting to get an idea of his persona and the rhythm to his speech, I attended ... and was delighted at the high entertainment value of his show. It was a fairly small venue, but Ron rocked it like it was Vegas.

Ron was also rather hands-on about his stories. He and Charles supplied one plot to me while I came up with a couple more on my own as well as a direction for the entire series. Fortunately, Ron agreed with my ideas, including the idea of his character doing all the wrong things, but always for the right reasons. He could alternately be triumphant and in the next adventure, be a victim of forces larger than he could conceive.

Also, Ron would rewrite my dialogue, so it sounded

more like what would come from the Master himself. At first, I honestly felt slightly perturbed by the number of corrections Ron made to my script. It didn't help that he was completely correct. Then he did fewer on the next. Soon, a script came back with no corrections at all. Needless to say, I was elated. Not only did I get "Ron" right, I had less work to do.

Plus, during this time, Ron and I had formed a mutual admiration society and I cherish his friendship and his dark, sticky sense of humor.

Then one day, Charles called me up to tell me he'd brought a new personality into the Silver Phoenix fold, Kadrolsha Ona (Carole). Kadrolsha was a former broadcaster as well as a psychic, a healer, an exorcist, and that didn't include her equestrian and military experience.

Me: "I'm the writer for Kadrolsha, right?"

Charles: "Who else could do her justice? Yes, you're the writer."

Me: "Oh, okay."

Aside from being a lady whose positivity could make you smile no matter how badly your day went, she was a woman of drive and a confidence that was contagious. Kinda like Mary Tyler Moore, who could turn the world on with her smile?

Kadrolsha was also the Real-Life Queen of the Paranormal. I have gone on record as saying she was the very first person – not just the first *woman* – to be a super-hero in real life and to have her own comic book. If there's another, let me know.

So that's why we had the last comics page in *THTOBG* featuring Kadrolsha. On one occasion, when Charles came to visit me at the Compound, I noticed that our lead story lacked our newest celebrity. So, without delay, I wrote a one-page addendum to our "We Have ..." in twenty minutes that gave the Queen of the Paranormal not just a reason to come to Bachelors Grove Cemetery in the first place, but to return.

And as Silver Phoenix Entertainment moved forward, more celebrities of the silver and small screens wanted to join the fun.

So, what's the key to breaking into independent comics writing, or drawing? It's wanting to do this thing, most of all. You must WANT to do this and not just as something to do, or a way to get your name out to the public, or a way to become (in)famous or wealthy (HAH!).

It's okay to write for the indies as a stepping stone towards the big money that the larger companies can pay. But don't count on your pet project becoming a Hollywood film because the major companies are mostly cherry-picking intellectual properties from The Big Two Comic Book Publishers because those characters will have some following.

Heck, creators used to write or draw comics because they thought it would put food on the table until they could score a job with an ad agency or writing books. Many of us take jobs in numerous fields with the intent of rising in the ranks in our field.

But you must have a desire to write for comics because you enjoy the challenges. You do it because you love seeing what the artist does with your words. You do it because you can get immediate feedback, and encouragement, from your readers.

You do this because it's fun, because it's a great way to meet others and forge friendships with creatives and fans alike. If that alone doesn't make this adventure worth taking, I don't know what will.

Every journey is best when shared with cool people.

Anyway, here's the first script ...

A Loser's Race

8 pages

By

Brian K. Morris

LOGLINE: A young track star hopes to catch the vanishing house, to prove that nothing and no one is speedier than him. However, no one is faster than death, especially death in its own front yard.

FORMAT and STYLE NOTES:

Despite what you might hear, there is NO official comic script format. What I use is a combination of formats that I've read over the years, primarily from a booklet entitled *The Comic Book Guide For the Artist * Writer * Letterer* produced in 1973 by Nicola Cuti for Charlton Comics. I wound up with a copy when I sent a script for a super-hero team-up title (a concept they never used, and I can't blame them) featuring characters the company no longer published. This 40-page pamphlet changed my life, literally.

In recent years, I modified this format based on feedback from writers Paul Kupperberg and Roger McKenzie concerning a script I submitted to the Charlton NEO publishing company. I enjoy the format's clarity, but I am not a stickler that everyone else employ it.

The scripts are initially broken down into printed pages (what the reader sees). This doesn't mean that a six-page script takes half a dozen pages to communicate its contents with the rest of the creative team. The script takes as long as it will take, period. Famously, Alan Moore's script for his classic *Watchmen* title is so packed with information that just describing the first panel takes a page and a half of written script.

I prefer to go for simpler descriptions instead of micromanaging my fellow creators, allowing them to bring their own contributions to the work. As I tell noob writers who take their cues from Alan Moore that only Alan Moore can get away with this type of scripting because he is Alan Moore. We can't because we are not Alan Moore.

Anyway, then the writer subdivides the pages into panels, each one to be filled with descriptions. The instructions for the artist(s), with potential color notes, are described first, followed by those for the letterer.

I try to use no more than six panels per page with 35 words (including captions and allowing for the extra room that sound effects (or SOUND FX) require. If I use fewer panels, I keep the total below 200 words for the entire page.

I place the number of panels each page will use to guide the artist and to make sure that the number of panels that I describe match the number of panels I claim to use at the top of the page. I don't describe a panel with a page break in the way. I will add CONTINUED, with a companion acknowledgment topping the next page.

For the record, the scripts presented in this book are pretty much as I submitted them to Silver Phoenix and Charles D. Moisant. The only major alterations I've executed have been in terms of the CONTINUED notations due to the original scripts being written on 8 ½ " by 11" paper and the 6" x 9" dimensions of this work.

The art descriptions usually focus on ONE focal point featuring ONE action. Detailing the background images do NOT involve mentioning the title of every book on a library shelf or fiddling with every microscopic detail. Unless I have a specific effect I want to see, I provide minimalist descriptions and allow the artists to contribute their share of the imagery.

After starting a script with a title page that provided the story's title, the finished page count, the logline (a one or two-sentence description of the story that could be used in promotion or catalog entries), and my contact information (name, street address, phone number, and e-mail address), I begin the script.

I capitalize the names of everyone in a panel so the artist knows just how many people to draw, unless it's a crowd scene. The script should be as easy for the artist to follow as the resulting story must be for the reader.

For the record, I frequently write my art descriptions first, often two or three pages at a stretch, and then go back and add the lettering instructions. This is to ensure that the visuals carry the lion's share of the storytelling responsibility. As a reader, you should be able to follow the basic plot of a comic story if the artists have done their job as storytellers properly.

To that end, I pay strict attention to body language and to denote facial expression in every panel where necessary.

In the credits, "TBD" stood for "To Be Determined." At the time I wrote the scripts, we had no idea who would illustrate, letter, or color the stories. In fact, I seem to recall that we toyed with the idea that the books might be black-

and-white as a cost-cutting measure. Or else I forgot to include the color artist in those early days.

You'll see some words are emphasized by the use of ALL CAPS. Many contemporary comic writers find this too reminiscent of an earlier, less sophisticated time. I figure it's part of the storytelling foundation that built this industry, so I use them, probably more than I should.

The shape of the word balloons could convey whether the voice or sound came through an electronic device (ELECTRONIC) or if the noise was loud (SHOUT) or soft (WHISPER) or if it had a spine-tingling timbre (EERIE). You will notice in some cases, sound effects and certain bits of dialogue are accompanied by instructions on where to put the tail, or the pointy part of the word balloon that should aim itself at the source of the sound.

Sound effects are usually placed near their source. And you'll see that I number all lettering inclusions per page while other writers who use this method might number all word balloons, captions, and sound effects in succession from the first page of the script to the last.

In recent years, letterers have added images to captions to denote who said the words since thought balloons (the cloud-like balloons with large dots as the tail that detailed what a character was thinking) seem to have fallen out of favor with many comic book writers. Me, I still love 'em when used appropriately.

"A Loser's Race" was written before I was reminded of the above fact. I claim full responsibility for my ignorance at the time.

The SPLASH panel is often the largest one on a page. This is often an image used to capture the reader's attention and often establishes the challenge that the protagonist must overcome during the course of the story.

Notice that I place, wherever possible, a brief description of each character upon their first appearance in the story. Some writers may use a separate page with more thorough detailing, just as playwrights would do, but this style works for me.

I also attempt to end each page with some bit of dialogue or a visual that demands the reader turn the page to find out what the result may be. Call it a mini-cliffhanger if you will. I certainly do.

You'll notice this first script is for an eight-page story. This was originally intended to be the first story in THTOBG #1, so it needed to introduce some of Charles' concepts and thus, a little more room for the story to breathe.

However, Charles elected to plot a story that introduced the vampires of Bachelors Grove instead and thus, THAT story became the anchor for our first issue. By the way, that story took ten pages, not eight, for me to tell. Go figure.

The following was my love letter to the classic EC Comics of my misspent youth with their great art and O'Henry-style endings. And as with the classic author, where else but in fiction can you expect the good guy to always escape and the bad guy to be punished commensurate with their crime?

PAGE ONE (FOUR PANELS)

PANEL ONE (SPLASH): Outdoors, daytime, the banner overhead declares MIDLOTHIAN HIGH TRACK & FIELD. The STARTER shoots his pistol and the race is on as TRENTON CALE (18, male, slender, long blonde hair, constant sneer) leaves the starter blocks, followed immediately by STEVE MALONE (17, clean-cut, brown curly hair, glasses) and three or four VARIOUS RUNNERS.

1 TITLE: A LOSER'S RACE

2 SOUND FX (PISTOL): BLAMM!

3 CAPTION (ELECTRONIC – it's the P.A. announcer): Next up in today's TRACK MEET is the 500-meter sprint. They're on the starting line and – THEY'RE OFF!

4 CREDITS: WRITTEN BY BRIAN K. MORRIS / ILLUSTRATED BY tbd / LETTERED BY tbd

PANEL TWO: TRENTON leads the pack as they head into the final stretch, STEVE hot on his heels with the VARIOUS RUNNERS lagging.

5 CAPTION (ELECTRONIC): Senior TRENTON CALE is the FAVORITE, as usual, and Junior STEVE MALONE is giving a good showing of himself. Look at those men RUN!

CONTINUED:

PAGE ONE CONTINUED:

PANEL THREE: A smiling STEVE breaks the tape across his chest with TRENTON's disappointment writing across his face.

6 CAPTION (ELECTRONIC): WOW! MALONE came from behind and is gonna TAKE the GOLD for this event. Trenton is silver, Penwright snags the bronze.

PANEL FOUR: In pain and sweating badly, TRENTON tries to catch his breath, glancing at a proud STEVE accepts his medal from the STARTER.

7 CAPTION (ELECTRONIC): As the MEDALS are being handed out, remember the 4-H is running the CONCESSIONS today so treat yourself. And remember NO ONE is a LOSER today.

PAGE TWO (FOUR PANELS)

PANEL ONE: Establishing shot of APOLLO'S COFFEEHOUSE in the daytime.

1 CAPTION: "Look at those losers ..."

PANEL TWO: STEVE is the humble center of attention from his MALE & FEMALE FRIENDS at one table, while TRENTON and GLENNA APPLE (17, cheerleader, wide-eyed, gorgeous) look at him from another.

2 GLENNA: Oh, lighten up, Trent. They're just CONGRATULATING Steve. Why so JEALOUS?

3 FRIEND: You were GREAT. You've gotta be the FASTEST BOY ALIVE.

PANEL THREE: On STEVE as he smilingly waves away his FRIENDS' comments.

4 FRIEND: Think you'll go PRO one day? Is the NEW KID gonna FORGET US when he's RICH?

5 STEVE: Heh, I'm just doing this for FUN. I'm not out to be FAMOUS.

CONTINUED:

PAGE TWO CONTINUED:

PANEL FOUR: TRENTON appears to be annoyed as he grabs GLENNA's arm painfully as she tries to leave the table.

> **6 TRENTON**: DAMMIT, winning doesn't even MEAN anything to him. And WHERE do you think YOU are going?

> **7 GLENNA**: I was just going to say congrat – OWCH! You're HURTING me!

> **8 TRENTON**: SIT DOWN, GLENNA. No, if you aren't WINNING –

PAGE THREE (FIVE PANELS)

PANEL ONE: In a locker room, TRENTON changes into his running gear while he's busy glaring at someone off-panel.

    1 CAPTION: "– then you're LOSING.   I don't like to LOSE. Neither should you."

    2 COACH (O.P.): GUYS, it's an important day for this team.

PANEL TWO: The COACH addresses the RUNNERS and STEVE listens intently while way in the background, TRENTON continues to stare angrily at Steve.

    3 RUNNER: Oh yeah? It's ALWAYS important. Like this is different HOW?

    4 COACH: Remember, we're a TEAM so we must support each other. There are no SUPERSTARS here.

                           CONTINUED:

PAGE THREE CONTINUED:

PANEL THREE: A RUNNER points to an embarrassed STEVE with a grin.

5 RUNNER: I bet Steve here's faster than a jackrabbit on expresso. Maybe even faster than the FARMHOUSE?

6 STEVE: Farmhouse? I've only lived here a couple of months. What's this farmhouse?

PANEL FOUR: The COACH rolls his eyes and smirks as he indicates the grinning RUNNER is flat-out nuts by making a circling motion around his ear.

7 COACH: Puh-LEASE! There's a local GRAVEYARD where some KOOKS say there's a GHOST FARMHOUSE. I guess the closer you get to it, it gets SMALLER until it's GONE.

8 RUNNER: I think someone's been reading too many SPOOKY COMIC BOOKS or drinking JAILHOUSE WINE.

CONTINUED:

PAGE THREE CONTINUED:

PANEL FIVE: On TRENTON as a cruel sneer takes over his features while staring at his off-panel rival.

    9 RUNNER (O.P.): But you gotta figure that with all that SMOKE being blown up someone's BACKSIDE, there might be a FIRE nearby.

    10 TRENTON (THOT): Hmm, forgot about that cemetery. That give me a SWEET, SWEET idea …

PAGE FOUR (FIVE PANELS)

PANEL ONE: At school, between classes, STEVEN has his locker open and reads an invitation.

> **1 CAPTION**: "Hi, Steve. I know what it's like to not have many friends. This is my way of making it up to you for –"

PANEL TWO: Inside the front room of his house, TRENTON turns towards the front door, his face contorted with anger, while he's holding the fearful RUNNER from the previous page by the front of his jacket. If there's a window in the scene, perhaps we could see the Moon to indicate that this is night time.

> **2 CAPTION**: "– not being very friendly. Meet me at my house and we'll crash a PARTY at my girl's. See you tomorrow night. Steve."

> **3 TRENTON**: You GET ME? You just SHUT the HELL UP and stick to MY PLAN. Otherwise, I DANCE on your KNEECAPS.

> **4 SOUND FX** (DOOR): NOK! NOK!

CONTINUED:

PAGE FOUR CONTINUED:

PANEL THREE: TRENTON is all smiles – the RUNNER in the background isn't, however – as he greets STEVE who waits on the front porch. From this point on, the story takes place at night.

> **5 RUNNER** (WHISPER): Y-yeah, Trenton … I get you … but I don't want to –

> **6 TRENTON**: STEVE! GREAT to see you, PAL! We'd better get RUNNING. Can't break TRAINING, you know.

PANEL FOUR: TRENTON leads STEVE, with the RUNNER bringing up the rear, away from his house and down the street.

> **7 TRENTON**: The PARENTS borrowed my CAR, but there's a SHORTCUT through one of the local TOURIST TRAPS we can take. Follow me.

> **8 STEVE**: HEY! SLOW DOWN! Don't KILL me before you get to know me! HA! HA!

PANEL FIVE: Establishing shot of the sign: ENTRANCE TO BACHELORS GROVE CEMETERY.

> **9 CAPTION**: "You're right, Steve. Our destination can certainly WAIT."

PAGE FIVE (FOUR PANELS)

PANEL ONE: Inside the graveyard, amidst the leaning and decaying tombstones, STEVE looks down to see the grass squishing with water as he runs amidst the leaning and decaying tombstones with the POND on one side, a grinning TRENTON on the other, and the RUNNER following nervously.

1 STEVE: What a MESS. That POND's rather FULL, isn't it? But it hasn't RAINED in WEEKS and the water STINKS.

2 TRENTON: She often OVERFLOWS when she's HUNGRY. Lots of BODIES at the bottom of her GULLET, so the stories say.

PANEL TWO: STEVE falls backwards into the POOL when TRENTON body checks him.

3 TRENTON: But there's always ROOM FOR ONE MORE! UGHHH!

4 SOUND FX: WHUMF!

5 STEVE (SHOUT): What the HELL! I'm FALLING! HELLLLP!

CONTINUED:

PAGE FIVE CONTINUED:

PANEL THREE: STEVE flails in the shallow POND as TRENTON watches with an evil leer. However, the RUNNER backs away in terror for what he's done.

> **6 STEVE** (SHOUT): HELLP! *glub Some – THING – PULLING ME DOWN! *gluub* GUYS! HELLLP!!!

> **7 SOUND FX** (WATER): SPLSSHSSHHHSSHH!!!

> **8 TRENTON**: HAH! THIS makes SURE that I'm the FASTEST guy ALIVE!

> **9 RUNNER**: NO! You were going to SCARE him. I didn't agree to MURDER! You're on your OWN!

PANEL FOUR: On TRENTON as he turns in the direction that the Runner already fled, surprise and wonder across his features.

> **10 TRENTON**: HEY! GET BACK HERE, you CHICKEN! I'm gonna pull him out after I SCARE him some –

> **11 TRENTON**: What the HELL is THAT?

PAGE SIX (FIVE PANELS)

PANEL ONE: TRENTON sees the FARMHOUSE and starts to run towards it.

1 TRENTON: A FARMHOUSE? HOH-LEE – I don't believe it's REAL. I can see the DOORWAY –

PANEL TWO: Outside GLENNA's house, the RUNNER is dead on his feet, but still slamming his fist upon the front door.

2 CAPTION: "– and I'm going IN!"

3 SOUND FX (KNOCKING): BOMP! BOMP!

4 GLENNA (SHOUT, FROM INSIDE): HOLD ON! I'M COMING!

PANEL THREE: GLENNA answers the door, but keeps the screen between herself and the RUNNER.

5 GLENNA: What? What are you –?

6 RUNNER: Glenna … *huff* … you've got … *huff* … got to help me …

CONTINUED:

PAGE SIX CONTINUED:

PANEL FOUR: Covered in sweat, his frantic eyes filled with tears, the RUNNER pleads with GLENNA who rolls her eyes in disbelief.

7 RUNNER: He pushed the new guy in the POND, leaving him to DROWN. You've got to HELP ME.

8 GLENNA: What a sick, SICK joke. Go play your pranks elsewhere.

PANEL FIVE: The door slams shut in the astonished RUNNER's face.

9 RUNNER: PLEASE! I can't stop your BOYFRIEND alone!

10 SOUND FX (DOOR): SLAMM!!!

11 GLENNA (THROUGH THE DOOR): DON'T SAY THAT! He's NOT my BOYFRIEND! GO AWAY!

PAGE SEVEN (SIX PANELS)

PANEL ONE: A nervous TRENTON looks at STEVE who lies face down in the POND.

> **1 TRENTON**: Don't go away ... oh, Lord ... DAMN ... NOOO! ... the bubbles STOPPED ... oh no ...

> **2 TRENTON**: I could dive in ... but the farmhouse ... bubbles stopped ... I'm looking at JAIL ... at the very least ... please SINK ...

PANEL TWO: TRENTON takes off towards the FARMHOUSE, STEVE and the POND now ignored.

> **3 TRENTON**: Aw, HELL! Steve's probably DEAD anyway. But before the COPS get me, I'm going to CATCH that FARMHOUSE! YOU HEAR ME?

PANEL THREE: The FARMHOUSE begins to recede from TRENTON's view as he races towards it at top speed, water from the POND splashing in his wake.

> **4 TRENTON** (SHOUT): NO! STOP SHRINKING! You are MINE! STOP! NOTHING is FASTER than ME! NOTHING!

CONTINUED:

PAGE SEVEN CONTINUED:

PANEL FOUR: On TRENTON as the veins in his neck bulge, sweat flies from him as he sprints, arms pumping frantically, wide-eyed, and desperate, his hands reaching forward in desperation.

> **5 TRENTON** (THOT): Unnhh … lungs burning … legs beyond tired … knees aflame … but can't stop … must not stop … only ONE chance …

PANEL FIVE: TRENTON makes a desperate leap forward towards the almost-vanished FARMHOUSE as the POND seems to rush up to catch the runner.

> **6 TRENTON** (SCREAM): AAHHRRRRGHHHH!!!

PANEL SIX: Close on TRENTON's fingertips as they clutch the base of the FARMHOUSE's bottom most porch step (or whatever the closest part of the house might be, like a doorway or what have you – whatever works best for you).

> **7 TRENTON** (SHOUT): GOTCHA! HA HA HA HA HA!

PAGE EIGHT (SIX PANELS)

PANEL ONE: TRENTON, triumphant albeit exhausted, pulls himself inside via the doorway of the FARMHOUSE, the physical world behind him.

1 TRENTON: HAH! CAUGHT YOU! I'm faster than LIGHT … even DEATH itself!

PANEL TWO: Shadows fall across TRENTON's face as he sees something off-panel that terrifies him enough that he loses his grip on the doorway.

2 TRENTON: And now to – WAIT! What are YOU? NO! STAY BACK! STAY –!

3 TRENTON (SHOUT): AIEEEEE!!!

PANEL THREE: GLENNA and the RUNNER are in the POND, tugging on STEVE's limp body, but the water almost refuses to release him. Glenna's looking at Steve, but something upwards and off-panel catches Runner's eye.

4 GLENNA: UHH! Can barely MOVE Steve. It's like the WATER won't let him GO!

5 STEVE (WEAK): *cough* uhhh *cough cough* glenna?

6 RUNNER: UGH! Glad you changed your mind, Glenna. We've got to – WAIT! What's THAT?

CONTINUED:

PAGE EIGHT CONTINUED:

PANEL FOUR: TRENTON's body hits the POND from high above, sending water everywhere and pushing STEVE, GLENNA, and the RUNNER out onto the cemetery grass.

7 SOUND FX (WATER): FLOOOOOSHHHH!!!

8 STEVE, GLENNA & RUNNER (SHARED SHOUT BALLOON): AAAAAHHHHH!!!

PANEL FIVE: GLENNA and the RUNNER watch as TRENTON's hand vanishes under the surface of the POND.

9 TRENTON (WEAK): HELLLP! Helllp. Helllllmmmph …

10 GLENNA: *gasp* She's taking TRENTON instead of STEVE.

11 RUNNER: "She?"

CONTINUED:

PAGE EIGHT CONTINUED:

PANEL SIX: STEVE opens his eyes while GLENNA and the RUNNER stare at the off-panel Pond. Her expression is cold hatred while the Runner's is pure horror.

12 STEVE (WEAK): yeah … "she" said … "thank you …" She's … a jealous wife indeed.

13 GLENNA: Yes … never race death on its home turf … you'll always LOSE.

14 CAPTION: THE END

A MOTHER'S LOVE

By

Brian K. Morris

LOGLINE: A woman has talked to her dead son almost every day for 20 years at his graveside. But when a horny stalker decides to cure her of her obsession, she finds her son has grown up to be a good man and a loyal defender.

"A Loser's Race" was immediately followed by "Mother's Love."

I worked for a cemetery for a year in the mid-Nineties as an assistant mortician. While I was there, I noticed a 30-something woman who made regular visits to a specific grave site. It seems she'd lost her infant son quite some time before.

At least once a week, this woman came out to her son's grave and talked to him, read stories to him, and treated him as if he was still listening and responding. Anyone who came close to her while she visited often left quickly, driven away by the woman's glare.

Stories abounded about the woman, told, and retold by the cemetery staff. Supposedly, she proved more talkative years before I worked there, and she shared part of her life with certain staffers. The woman's fixation over her loss apparently drove her husband and the rest of her family away.

No one knew what she did for a living, but she regularly showed up around the same time every Tuesday afternoon, and sometimes on more than one evening. She frequently brought new books and toys for her son. Apparently, the afterlife could become boring without some kind of entertainment and it beat letting the boy watch television all the time.

And once the sunset began, the woman collected her toys and books, folded the blanket she rested upon, then drove back to her everyday life.

If you looked hard enough, as closely as you could without interrupting them, you would see the mother listen to words of love from a phantom who could never leave her mind … or her heart.

PAGE ONE (3 PANELS)

PANEL ONE (SPLASH): As the sun goes down at the edge of Bachelors Grove Cemetery, ROD (twenties, male, punk biker wannabe) stares from behind a gnarled old tree at EMILY CATERS (middle aged, long dark hair, very attractive) who kneels down at the foot of a specific grave, one hand on the grass, and it looks like she's talking to whoever is buried inside.

1 CAPTION: LOVE never ends, not even when the target of that affection DIES. However, there is a SPECIAL type of love, a powerful devotion, that when mixed with OBSESSION, creates one of the most unstoppable forces in the universe.

2 TITLE: A MOTHER'S LOVE

3 ROD: Mmm … yeah, I'm paying attention. I always pay attention, baby.

4 CREDITS: BRIAN K. MORRIS – WRITER / TBD – ILLUSTRATOR / TBD – LETTERER

PANEL TWO: EMILY smiles as she continues to talk to the grave with ROD hiding in the background, watching.

5 ROD: Lookit her … BLABBING AWAY to that HEADSTONE … she's NUTS like my MA, but she's way STACKED.

6 GINGER (SHOUT, O.P.): HEY! ROD!

CONTINUED:

PAGE ONE CONTINUED:

PANEL THREE: ROD whirls around angrily and we now see that GINGER (late teens, blonde, goth) angrily points at the man.

7 GINGER: Did you FORGET I'm your old lady? Whatcha checkin' out someone's MOM for? 'Specially THAT crazy cow.

8 ROD: HER? You know so much, GINGER, what's up with HER?

PAGE TWO (6 PANELS)

PANEL ONE: GINGER stands to one side of a FLASHBACK vision to EMILY lying in the hospital bed, proudly cradling her BABY in her arms as her HUSBAND leans down to inspect his child.

> **1 GINGER**: If you were LOCAL, you'd know. She used to be my SITTER It's kinda SAD.

> **2 CAPTION** (OVER EMILY'S HALF OF THE PANEL): "EMILY CARTLAND had a sweet husband and a terrific life about twenty years ago. Then they had a son they called TAB, like that old film actor."

PANEL TWO: In this FLASHBACK panel, with tears and madness welling in her eyes, EMILY holds up her unbreathing baby as her HUSBAND reacts in horror.

> **3 CAPTION**: "But they didn't know as much about CRIB DEATH like we do now. She found little Tab … not breathing … so still … she loved him more than life … she couldn't stop screaming for him to wake up …"

PANEL THREE: In this FLASHBACK panel, EMILY stares wide-eyed at the baby's burial site, ignoring her HUSBAND who's holding her as well as the PRIEST administering the last rites.

> **4 CAPTION**: "But it wasn't just the baby that died … something inside Emily died too …"

CONTINUED:

PAGE TWO CONTINUED:

PANEL FOUR: In this FLASHBACK, EMILY smiles as she talks to the headstone while her HUSBAND tries in vain to pull her away.

5 CAPTION: "Emily came back to talk to Tab's grave … actually, her baby inside … first it was once a week for an hour … then every day … then two hours a day … soon, her husband would have to drag her back home …

6 CAPTION: "Eventually, he gave up trying … the divorce was uncontested … she probably doesn't know her man moved on …"

PANEL FIVE: In this FLASHBACK, in the dead (so to speak) of winter, EMILY sits in a chair, happily reading to the headstone, alone … but she doesn't seem to care.

7 CAPTION: "She never dated again. Just goes to work for my dad in the morning, comes straight here to read to her … her baby … every day … until the sun goes down …"

PANEL SIX: Back in the present, GINGER shrugs while ROD takes a pull from a beer, leering at the off-panel Emily.

8 GINGER: Losing a kid … I can't even imagine … but I feel for her.

9 ROD: Yeah, I'd feel for her too … given half a chance.

PAGE THREE (4 PANELS)

PANEL ONE: GINGER slugs ROD hard enough to knock him backwards.

1 SOUND FX (SLAP): SLAPP!

2 GINGER: YOU PIG! You too STUPID DRUNK to – oh, I GIVE UP! You're always IGNORING what's right in front of you for something you CAN'T HAVE!

PANEL TWO: As GINGER storms out of the panel, ROD pulls himself up drunkedly.

3 GINGER: I've had enough! GOODBYE! DROP DEAD, you rotten DRUNK!

4 ROD (WEAK): huh-hey … no one duz dat to rod … nuh wun … *buuuurp*

PANEL THREE: EMILY sits cross-legged at her son's grave, reading happily from a hardcover book.

5 EMILY: You've come a long way, my beautiful son. I read Uncle Bumbly Bunny like a blink of an eye ago. Now, you're doing college-level courses. Mommy is SO proud of you.

CONTINUED:

PAGE THREE CONTINUED:

PANEL FOUR: EMILY still reads as ROD stumbles from behind his place of concealment towards her, a look of drunken lust across his face.

> **6 EMILY**: Of course, you'll ALWAYS be my little boy, sleeping in my arms, getting you ready for school, teaching you how to tie your –"

PAGE FOUR (5 PANELS)

PANEL ONE: EMILY is startled by ROD who towers over her menacingly.

1 EMILY: OH! You STARTLE.D me. I'm sorry, but this is private between me and my son, please.

2 ROD: Uh-huh, I'm all about doing things … in private.

PANEL TWO: EMILY turns back to the gravestone and begins reading again while ROD leers down at her.

3 EMILY: Now, where were we? As I was saying, many scholars think the American Civil War was only about slavery, but it also included –

PANEL THREE: ROD runs his fingers through EMILY's hair, an act that seems to nauseate her.

4 ROD: C'mon babe … don't ignore me … hear it's been a long time … probably need it bad, huh?

5 EMILY: EWW!!! Get AWAY from us. You make my skin crawl. Please LEAVE.

CONTINUED:

PAGE FOUR CONTINUED:

PANEL FOUR: From behind the tree where Rod hid, a FIGURE (male, handsome, 20-year old ... okay, it's TAB) watches ROD laugh at EMILY.

> **6 ROD**: US? Lady, your son is DEAD! You've spent all this time talkin' to nothin' but DIRT and WORMS and BONES. But now you got ME, babe.

PANEL FIVE: EMILY weeps as she presses her fists over her ears, which amuses ROD as he sadistically leans down to yell at her.

> **7 EMILY** (SHOUT): NOOO! GO AWAY! HE'S NOT DEAD! HE'S NOT DEAD!

> **8 ROD**: CRAZY BROAD! Good thing DOCTOR ROD'S got a POCKET MONSTER to bring you back to your SENSES ... and you'll LOVE it, doncha know?

> **9 TAB** (SHOUT FROM O.P.): You heard the lady ... GET LOST!

PAGE FIVE (5 PANELS)

PANEL ONE: ROD has a handful of EMILY's hair and looks around frantically as he drags the woman by her hair away from the grave and towards the tree.

> **1 ROD**: HUH? WHO SAID THAT? Rod can have whatever ... WHOEVER ... he wants ... and nobody's gonna stop –

> **2 TAB** (O.P.): Were you listening, SLUG? I said GET LOST.

PANEL TWO: TAB stands at the foot of the GRAVE and in his surprise, ROD drop EMILY.

> **3 TAB**: Or are you DEAF as well as STUPID, SMELLY, and FUGLY?

> **4 ROD**: WHUH? Who the hell are YOU?

PANEL THREE: TAB points accusingly at ROD who pulls out a knife from his belt as he charges the young man.

> **5 TAB**: I'm this woman's GUARDIAN ANGEL. So leave her be or suffer the painful CONSEQUENCES.

> **6 ROD**: Consequences? I'll show you CONSEQUENCES. You're DEAD, man.

CONTINUED:

PAGE FIVE CONTINUED:

PANEL FOUR: To his astonishment, ROD's knife passes through a smiling TAB, specifically his arm.

7 ROD: Gunna CUT you – WHUH?

8 TAB: You aren't cutting ME, and do you think I'd let you touch HER?

PANEL FIVE: TAB brushes ROD's arm away as he punches the punk hard enough to not only disarm him, but send him flying backwards towards the grave.

9 TAB: Over MY DEAD BODY!

10 SOUND FX (PUNCH): KRAK!

11 ROD (SHOUT): OWCH!

PAGE SIX (6 PANELS)

PANEL ONE: TAB's grave opens up and ROD struggles to exit it – however, TAB stands over him, breaking his arms and legs, almost folding the punk in on himself.

1 CAPTION: "The cemetery is FULL … but I think I can SQUEEZE you IN."

2 ROD (SCREAM): AAAHHH!!! HELP ME!!!

3 SOUND FX (ROD'S BONES & SCREAMS): KRENCH! KRAKK! AIEEEE! ARGHHH! SNAPP!

PANEL TWO: As the sod closes over ROD, his broken, twisted hands desperately clawing at the freedom he'll never see again, TAB grabs EMILY's shoulders with a loving smile.

4 ROD (MUFFLED): mmmf! mmf! mmm … *!

5 TAB: He will never bother you again.   Are you okay? Please say you are.

6 EMILY: I'm fine, I'm fine. But who are –? *gasp* GOOD LORD!

CONTINUED:

PAGE SIX CONTINUED:

PANEL THREE: EMILY, her eyes wide with tears and joyous surprise, recognizes TAB.

>**7 EMILY**: TAB? It CAN'T be you! How is it you are so … so … GROWN UP? I thought spirits can't AGE.

>**8 TAB**: Most don't, but I did. It's all thanks to YOU, MOM.

PANEL FOUR: TAB and EMILY embrace each other tightly.

>**9 TAB**: Kids don't GROW just because you FEED them or BUY them things. We are all SEEDS that your love NURTURES, even after we pass on.

>**10 TAB**: You SAVED me from becoming just another SPIRIT. I'm TRULY ALIVE. I have the BEST MOM ever. I LOVE YOU!

PANEL FIVE: EMILY hugs TAB so, so tightly, her eyes closed and contentment spreading over her face as happy tears flow down her cheeks.

>**10 EMILY**: Now that I see you, it's like MADNESS has lifted from my MIND. I LOVE YOU too, Tab. Please come home with me.

>**11 TAB**: I wish I could. The unbreakable RULES demand I stay. However …

CONTINUED:

PAGE SIX CONTINUED

PANEL SIX: FLASH FORWARD: Bundled against the winter, a silver-haired EMILY sits on a small stool at the foot of her son's grave and reads from a book while TAB sits at the foot of his own plot, cheerfully listening.

12 CAPTION: "… I'll be here FOREVER as long as you want to visit me, Mom."

13 EMILY: What shall I read to you today, Tab?

14 TAB: Anything you want, Mom. Anything at all.

15 CAPTION: NEVER TRULY THE END

GONE IN 666 SECONDS

By

Brian K. Morris
Based on a story idea by
Charles D. Moisant

LOGLINE: When the accelerator hits 666 while driving by Bachelors Grove Cemetery, it's a white-knuckle ride to Hell.

One of my pleasures in working with Charles is one-upping him.

Early on, he suggested we collaborate on some stories. Granted, this was with the caveat that I could still plot some stories on my own, to which he agreed eagerly.

As has been mentioned, Charles is quite dyslexic so reading and writing are a challenge for him at times. Besides, when he and I talk out a story, he spits out a wild concept which I try to push to the next level. Then I'll show him a script based on our conversations and see if I can make him laugh with my audacious attempt to exceed him.

One night, Charles called me to tell me about a story idea he devised where any automobile that drives past Bachelors Grove Cemetery when its odometer hit 666 miles would be visited by demons and it had one minute to hit the six hundred and sixty-seven mark or else dire stuff would occur to the car's occupants. We'll ignore the physics involved for the sake of our story, all right?

Well, now it was up to me to ramp up the cruelty. I live for Charles' laughter as he cries out, "Oh, my God!" with every new surprise I give him.

And notice by now, I left room for the colorist credit. II was also becoming more thorough concerning telling the letterer where the sound effects are to be placed. I like to think I'm evolving as a writer when I did that. If nothing else, my scripts grew more creator-friendly.

PAGE ONE (4 PANELS)

PANEL ONE: On a summer night, under the light of a half moon, the family station wagon ('60s vintage) drives slowly by Bachelors Grove Cemetery, its headlights casting twin beams down on the asphalt two-lane road.

>**1 CAPTION** (OMNISCIENT): The late Fifties in Midlothian, Illinois. Elvis is in the Army, rock 'n' roll sweeps the nation, and everybody still likes Ike.

>**2 SINGING** (FROM CAR): SHE'LL BE COMIN' 'ROUND THE MOUNTAIN WHEN SHE COMES, WHEN SHE COMES –

>**3 CAPTION** (OMNISCIENT): But not all is truly well. Not tonight.

PANEL TWO: Inside the car, DAD (early 30s, dressed in a white shirt and necktie) smiles as he looks in the rear-view mirror while driving. Beside him, MOM (late 20s, blonde, hairstyle – think Sue Storm from the early *Fantastic Four* – pillbox hat, conservative dress that will come below her knees when we see it later) checks her makeup in her compact's mirror. In the back seat, SIS (seven years old, a younger version of her mom except her hair is up in pigtails and she's wearing a school uniform) plays with her stuffed doggie while the SON (ten years old, freckles, resembles his father, striped shirt, and coonskin hat) stares out the window, bored with the family DOG (a mutt, basically) licks the boy's ear.

CONTINUED:

PAGE ONE CONTINUED:

4 RADIO (ELECTRONIC): And that's CONWAY TWITTY, still MAKIN' BELIEVE. It's almost MIDNIGHT here at Radio 890 and – * BZZZT *

5 MOM: Sorry the bridge party went long. Gosh, and on a school night too.

6 DAD: S'alright, honey. We're almost home.

7 RADIO (ELECTRONIC): That's right, folks –

PANEL THREE (SPLASH): Surprised, DAD's hand stops just inches from the AM radio's volume dial as he and MOM look at each other with astonishment.

8 RADIO (ELECTRONIC): – DON'T TOUCH THAT DIAL! Think FAST or else you and your entire family will be –

9 TITLE: GONE IN 666 SECONDS!

10 CREDITS: CO-PLOT/WRITER: BRIAN K. MORRIS – ARTIST(S): TBD – LETTERER: TBD – COLORIST: TBD – STORY IDEA/EDITOR: CHARLES D. MOISANT

PANEL FOUR: Close on odometer – the analog reading is 000666.0 – NO OTHER DIALOG OR CAPTIONING.

PAGE TWO (6 PANELS)

PANEL ONE: SIS and SON lean forward, gripping the edge of the back seat, as DAD begins to nervously sweat, and MOM touches her husband's arm with concern.

1 MOM: What kind of crazy radio show is this? It's not like that MARS INVASION, is it?

2 RADIO (ELECTRONIC): Glad you asked, BLONDIE.

PANEL TWO: On SIS and SON in the back seat of the car. She shrugs her shoulders while he pets the DOG who chews on the boy's shirt.

3 RADIO (ELECTRONIC, O.P.): ANY vehicle that passes BACHELORS GROVE CEMETERY when their ODOMETER hits THE MARK OF THE BEAST, is CURSED for the next MILE!

4 SON (WHISPER): Big deal …

5 RADIO (ELECTRONIC, O.P.): But first, a VERY SPECIAL GUEST!

CONTINUED:

PAGE TWO CONTINUED:

PANEL THREE: A DEMON wearing the scraps of a human disguise around its face and shoulders, slams against the windshield, startling DAD and MOM.

> **6 SOUND FX** (DEMON HITTING THE WINDSHIELD): WHUMPHH!

> **7 DAD &MOM** (SHOUT): AAAHHH!

> **8 DEMON** (EERIE): OWCH! GOLLY! That STINGS like HECK, DARN IT!

> **9 RADIO** (ELECTRONIC, O.P.): Straight from the bowels of HELL, welcome your own personal soul-shredding DEMON!*

> **10 CAPTION** (OMNISCIENT): *EDITOR'S NOTE: A demon's true visage is so HORRIFYING that the sight would KILL a normal human.

PANEL FOUR: MOM closes her eyes and prays fearfully as DAD grimly concentrates on his driving, looking past the leering DEMON.

> **11 MOM** (WHISPER): – I pray the Lord my soul to keep –

> **12 DEMON** (EERIE): You BETTER hold onto it TIGHT, Toots. Oh, Dad, in case you are CONCERNED, I'm not here to RAPE your SOULS. Not TONIGHT, at least.

CONTINUED:

PAGE TWO CONTINUED:

PANEL FIVE: The DEMON laughs and points past DAD and MOM who turn with horror towards the off-panel back seat.

13 DEMON (EERIE): No, I just wanted the BEST SEAT in the HOUSE for the REAL SHOW.

PANEL SIX: Close on odometer – the analog reading is 000666.2 – NO OTHER DIALOG OR CAPTIONING.

PAGE THREE (5 PANELS)

PANEL ONE: A terrified MOM reaches towards SIS and SON. Outside the window and clinging to the rear window are several different DEMONS (all horrible, even under their flesh masks). The little girl's eyes are wide with wonder as she reaches for the window crank. In response, the Daughter's brother looks at his sister with disgust. The DOG recoils at the sight of more DEMONS on his owner's side of the car.

1 MOM: NO! DON'T TOUCH THAT!

2 SIS: Are you clowns? You aren't funny.

3 DEMON OUTSIDE WINDOW (EERIE): No, we're #&K&@$ SANTA, okay? Let us IN, little girl.

PANEL TWO: DEMONS pour into the back seat, overwhelming SIS and the SON as one reaches over the seat to seize MOM while DAD keeps his terror-widened eyes on the road ahead.

4 SOUND FX (DEMONS): RRRRAAUGHH!!!

5 MOM (SCREAM): AIEEE!

6 SIS (SHOUT): DADDY! HELP MM—PHHH!

7 DAD (WHISPER): How does this nightmare end? What can I do? Lord, what do I do?

CONTINUED:

PAGE THREE CONTINUED:

PANEL THREE: The DEMON leers at DAD through the windshield, scratching an upside-down crucifix in the glass with a talon. Sweat pours down the nervous father's face while he grips the wheel tightly.

8 DEMON (EERIE): First, leave HIM out of this. Breaking the curse is simple … all you need to do is reach one mile beyond SATAN'S AREA CODE. It's EASY … do ya WANNA?

9 DAD (SHOUT): YES! ANYTHING!

PANEL FOUR: DAD is surprised when his SON's hands – now claws – wrap around his throat.

10 DEMON (EERIE, O.P.): Oh-KAY! But it's not as EASY as I hinted … as you'll see.

11 DEMON (EERIE, O.P.): I think your BOY has a GRIP on the situation … and something OBSCENE to say about it.

PANEL FIVE: Close on odometer – the analog reading is 000666.4 – NO OTHER DIALOG OR CAPTIONING.

PAGE FOUR (5 PANELS)

PANEL ONE: The SON digs his talons into DAD's windpipe, choking him and drawing a tiny bit of blood. SIS watches her brother with wide-eyed ecstasy as she pulls the doll's head from the rest of its body. Behind each child is a DEMON, each one pulling on glowing strings as if the children were puppets.

> **1 SIS** (EERIE): DO IT … tear Daddy's throat out … I want to finger paint with his BLOOD.

> **2 SON** (EERIE): You WORK too hard … never play CATCH … never come to PTA meetings … never show me your PLAYBOY MAGAZINES … I HATE YOU!!!

> **3 DAD** (WEAK): * gurgle * Son … you're … choking … please … stop …

PANEL TWO: The DEMON on the automobile hood smiles evilly at the off-panel Dad as the supernatural entity crooks a thumb towards the roadside speed limit sign.

> **4 ROAD SIGN**: SPEED LIMIT 30 MPH

> **5 DEMON** (EERIE): Hey, just get to 667 and you're HOME FREE. That's the GOOD NEWS.

> **6 DEMON** (EERIE): The BAD NEWS is it'll take FOREVER at this speed. Getting a SPEEDING TICKET and LOSING YOUR SOUL on the same night would SUCK.

CONTINUED:

96

PAGE FOUR CONTINUED:

PANEL THREE: DAD reacts with horror as his WIFE leans over, licking the sweat from her husband's cheek. Her wrists and throat are wrapped with the necromantic strings and her appearance is more like a hooker than a stay-at-home Fifties housewife.

7 CAPTION (DEMON, EERIE): "Plus, you'll find there are some delicious DISTRACTIONS."

8 WIFE (EERIE): Listen … BOY … let me tell you about my fantasies … the ones I use to block out the taste of your KISSES.

9 DAD (WHISPER): No … please let them go … I'll do anything …

PANEL FOUR: The DEMON on the car's hood slams his fist against the windshield, leaving a lattice-work of cracked glass, some of which spills onto DAD, landing in his eyes and forcing him to wince.

10 DEMON (EERIE): NO! You will PLAY THE GAME, mortal! Keep your EYES on the ROAD and DRIVE!

PANEL FIVE: Close on odometer – the analog reading is 000666.7.

11 CAPTION (DEMON): "While you await DAMNATION!"

PAGE FIVE (6 PANELS)

PANEL ONE: With new-found resolve, DAD shrugs hard, forcing MOM, SIS, and SON away, giving him a moment's respite. He grips the wheel hard.

> **1 DAD**: You want driving, I'll GIVE you DRIVING! Hang on TIGHT, demon. We're going to HELL together!

PANEL TWO: On DAD's shoe (a brown penny loafer) as it presses hard, pinning the accelerator to the floor.

> **2 SOUND FX** (ENGINE): VAH-ROOOM!!!

PANEL THREE: The DEMON digs his claws into the hood to remain in place as the car races down the road. DAD's eyes reflect his fury as MOM, SIS, and the SON stare hatefully at the man behind the wheel.

> **3 DEMON** (EERIE): You think driving FASTER will end your TORMENT? Like you're the FIRST to THINK of that?

> **4 DEMON** (EERIE): I say TAKE YOUR TIME … smell the roses, FEEL the TALONS of FEAR!

> **CONTINUED**:

PAGE FIVE CONTINUED:

PANEL FOUR: On DAD as he rears his head back, screaming in mortal agony.

    5 DAD: A few more seconds and we'll be free of –

    6 DAD (SCREAM): ARRGGHHH!

PANEL FIVE: The accelerator now takes on the shape of a hand with DAD's foot pressed hard into the unearthly palm. The claws dig deeply, painfully into the father's foot, piercing the leather of his shoe.

    7 CAPTION (DEMON): "STUPID FINITE BEING!   Do you believe a demon can only possess HUMANS?

    8 CAPTION (DEMON): "Never had an accelerator PUSH BACK?"

PANEL SIX: Close on odometer – the analog reading is 000666.8 and the last dial creeps towards 000666.9.

    9 CAPTION (DEMON): "Prepare to spend ETERNITY suffering in HELL.

    10 CAPTION (DEMON): "So close, so far away … so unfair … SO WHAT? HA HA HA!

PAGE SIX (5 PANELS)

PANEL ONE: DAD fearfully resists MOM's powerful attempt to pull her husband's mouth closer for a kiss. Her eyes are dark and lustful, her teeth are pointed, and her tongue spews from her mouth takes on the shape of a snake's.

1 MOM (EERIE): You FAILED me in EVERY way as a HUSBAND … lift your foot from the gas pedal and PERHAPS I won't HATE you forever …

2 DAD: NO! I will SAVE YOU and our CHILDREN. To HELL with FAILURE!

PANEL TWO: Close on odometer – the analog reading is 000667.0.

3 CAPTION (DAD): "And I'll never let you down ever again."

4 SOUND FX: SKREEECH!

5 DEMON (EERIE, O.P., NO BALLOON): NNNOOOOO!!!

CONTINUED:

PAGE SIX CONTINUED:

PANEL THREE: The sun begins to rise in the ease as the car rests on the side of the road. The windshield is smashed, there are indentations on the hood, and all four doors are open, allowing the NUMEROUS DEMONS to flee back towards the cemetery gates.

> **6 RANDOM DEMON** (EERIE): The LIGHT! FLEE to the CEMETERY!

> **7 ANOTHER RANDOM DEMON** (EERIE): Until NEXT time, meatbags!

> **8 STILL ANOTHER RANDOM DEMON** (EERIE): There is ALWAYS a next time!

PANEL FOUR: DAD clutches the steering wheel, his eyes dark, grim, and hard as he stares straight ahead into Eternity. MOM is back to normal, but her tears of regret make her mascara run. SIS tearfully clutches her decapitated doll to her heart while the SON hugs the family DOG.

> **9 MOM**: I'm s-so sorry. I don't know what got into me. I didn't mean –

> **10 DAD** (CHILLY): Shut the hell up, woman.

> **11 SIS**: I want to go home, Daddy. Please take us home.

> **12 SON**: It's over … right?   They won't come back ever again, will they?

CONTINUED:

PAGE SIX CONTINUED:

PANEL FIVE: Close on the DOG as it sits on the SON's lap. The innocent canine eyes are now very human, very conniving, very evil as the mutt stares at the reader.

13 SON: I mean they're gone for good, right? Dad?

14 SON: DAD?

15 CAPTION: THE END …

WE HAVE ...

By

Brian K. Morris

Based on a plot by **Charles D. Moisant**

"We have to put this in," said Charles.

"No, we don't!" Brian replied.

Yeah, that's how a lot of our planning sessions go.

Charles D. Moisant is a hand grenade of ideas. Like me, he can't hear a plot idea without adding to it or changing it. Get the two of us together, it's a concept tsunami.

On the other hand, I'm the guy who believes in elevator pitches and less is more. I frequently tell him that he might want to stop "over selling" a title. This came to a head when he revealed the ending of a comic I plan on writing to a potential customer. "Now he doesn't need to buy the issue. You just told him how it ended." Charles has been a good boy ever since, at least around me.

And yes, I do have a history of bossing my bosses around. No doubt, this explains why I'm a freelancer now.

Anyway, sometimes it's a mess as we each fight for plotting supremacy. But often, I have to remember that it's Charles' original story and the entire series is his idea anyway. Besides, he's paying for it ("Every damn day," one is tempted to reply.)

On the other hand, I'm not paid to transcribe Charles' scripts. He didn't bring me aboard to be a passive member of the team. I like surprising him with what I bring to his story.

We're remarkably on the same page in so many ways while being as yin-and-yang as can be. Story wise, we both want to amuse and astound our readers as much as we want to please ourselves. We want to write what no one is really writing for us.

He often phones me to tell me about his most recent story idea and we hammer it out between us. Or one of us will visit the other – we live three hours apart – and the story ideas start to fly. Some notions head towards the clouds and in all honesty, some burrow themselves into the ground, never to surface again.

Also, some of Charles' ideas are just one-sentence notions that he leaves to me to flesh out. This is one of the few that he gives me that are intricately plotted. Since I enjoy adding to the story, when Charles' ideas become a little too packed for me to the point where I have little or no room to contribute, I ask him to write it himself. Despite his dyslexia, he can make some scripting magic happen when he's motivated.

As mentioned earlier, I wrote "A Loser's Race" to give a gentle introduction to the Bachelors Grove universe. Then Charles decided he wanted something a bit stronger to lead into his vampire concept. So, he came up with the plot for "We Have ..."

Charles' original title was one word longer. Read the last panel and you'll know that third word was. However, I felt that using that word on the splash page would render the story anti-climactic. I suggested we only use 66.6% (naturally) of it so there's a "ta-dah" moment on page eight for the reader.

The basic narrative structure for the story was mine. I dug writing the opening, adding a little bit of sensuality to the story, which I kinda had to abandon in order to get all of Charles' ideas in.

One added benefit of this story is that it reminded me, as an editor, that these stories needed at least one human interaction with the scary stuff by at least halfway through. Also, the protagonist(s) had to *react* to the challenge, whether it was reflected in the dialogue, the captions, the facial expressions, or the body language. These fictional constructs, the "everymen" and everywomen," are the readers' entry point to the story and their reactions assist in guiding the readers' own internal responses.

At the time I wrote the original script, Charles plan for *THTOBG* was to feature Goth illusionist Master Ron Fitzgerald as the regular feature, much in the way that many DC and Marvel anthology titles of the Silver Age featured one main character, followed by non-related stories. Also, Charles hadn't detailed his plans for Lilith Yager. In fact, at this point in time, Charles chose writer Linda Lee King to script Lilith and I was trying to train her how to script comics.

It worked out that Linda Lee would turn her attention to a Lilith novel in order to bring about plot elements I felt were just a tad too intense for a PG-13 comic book, thus I would eventually take on the writing chores myself.

Then Kadrolsha Ona (Carole) joined our lineup, as you read earlier. A real-life psychic and healer, as well as the very first Real Life Super-Hero to get her own comic book,

Kadrolsha was going to get her own title, a companion to *THTOBG*. And then Charles changed his mind.

Charles: "You know how you wrote Kadrolsha's stories so they'd all go into one issue?"

Me: "Yeah. Why?"

Charles: "She's now going to be in the *Bachelors Grove* comic along with Ron."

Me: "I thought Ron was our main feature."

Charles: "So is Kadrolsha now. And so is Lilith."

Me: "You realize you have only 23 pages to fill and this will take up most of the book?"

Charles: "You'll make it work. I know you will."

Me: "Oh, okay."

Since Kadrolsha was going to be in *THTOBG*, I concocted a one-page script, an addendum to "We Have ..." This would introduce Kadrolsha as well as Lilith, giving the former a reason to revisit Bachelors Grove Cemetery.

Now that the stars were in alignment, both in the skies and in our comic book, the stories were assigned. "A Loser's Race" was given to my friend and *Purple Claw* collaborator, Claudio Cordeiro. However, Charles decided our collaboration on "We Have ..." should launch our cemetery empire.

Charles selected artist Vagner Fernandez to illustrate the inaugural story. I'd never heard of the man but when Charles sent me a fresh page, my pulse raced. His work was exciting, his linework clean, and his storytelling ability was on the beam.

However, due to the press of other priorities, I didn't take the time to edit/check the artwork arriving, same with Charles. About 2/3rds of the way through the story, I started wondering why elements that I felt needed emphasis weren't getting their proper focus in the art.

Then I checked on page 7 of the story, looking at the trio of spirits who helped Sally. The original plan was to take three characters Charles had created: an Egyptian male who was over three millennia dead, someone from around the time of the American Revolutionary War, and the third man would be less than a century past. All of these new people came from a model sheet that Charles had prepared, and I wrote up a description of all three men that would go into a *Bachelors Grove* "bible" for other writers to use.

Upon seeing the Indian brave on the page, my frantic question to Charles was, "Who the hell is that?"

A couple of e-mails later, Charles learned that Vagner ran my scripts through Google Translate, which could be remarkably accurate. It could also be as useful as taking a lawn mower into a mine field. Rather than find someone in the Chicago area who could translate my story accurately for Vagner, I decided to go back and rewrite the captions as necessary. I also had to make up a name for the new character.

One consideration was that at least a year passed between the time when I completed the first draft of this script and when I had to rewrite it for print. Believe me, I was grateful that the rewrite was as easy, and as brief, as it turned out to be. And now we had one more character to play with.

Of course, it was a study in contrasts between Charles and myself. When I discovered the variations in my scripts, I admittedly went nuclear. I believe I also quit the company over the artwork errors at that point (Charles talked me back in, naturally). Anyway, Charles told me to calm down and convinced me to re-do the script to accommodate the new arrival and everything would be fine.

And then once the coloring came in …

Charles: "I have to contact the colorist. And you have to rewrite your script."

Me: "Okay, I'll bite. Why?"

Charles: "Because your dialogue for my character, Lilith, is far too emotional. She needs to have a neutral voice, no emotion."

Me: "Sure. Whatever. And what's up with the colorist?"

Charles: "He gave Lilith the wrong color of eyes. It's vital that they be the right color."

Me: (sighing) "Oh, okay."

Not knowing Deron Bennett, our amazing letterer yet, I felt compelled to add one bit of direction under the logline on the first page of my script:

NOTE TO THE LETTERER:
SOME OF THE CAPTIONS CONTAINED WITHIN
WILL BE NARRATED BY A DIFFERENT SPEAKER
AND BE NOTED IN THE DESCRIPTION.
THE ONLY ABBREVIATION WILL BE
"OMNI" FOR THE OMNISCIENT SPEAKER.
ANY OTHER QUESTIONS, FEEL FREE TO ASK
ME OR CHARLES. AND THANK YOU!

For the completists among you, the following is the original approved script for "We Have ..." You'll get to see the third soul that originally was to appear to Sally. Consider it a bonus.

PAGE ONE (3 PANELS)

PANEL ONE (SPLASH): One night, SALLY KREZWRENKLE (17, blonde, see model sheet) emerges from THE HOUSE almost at a run as she wipes tears from her eyes.

1 TITLE: WE HAVE …

2 CAPTION/OMNI: This wasn't how the party was supposed to be. Wearing clothing she'd concealed from her mother's notice, she accepted the invitation from the girls who mocked her at lunch and cheerleading practice when her gaze was averted.

3 CAPTION/OMNI: She was supposed to be fawned over for once, accepted for being as edgy as any of her classmates. Then out came the illegal alcohol and the pills …

4 CAPTION/OMNI: Wanted in unwanted ways, touched by strangers, ridiculed by so-called friends, she ran through the nearest exit into the last night of her life.

5 SALLY (THOT): WHAT? The address was on 98th Street? Where am I NOW?

CONTINUED:

PAGE ONE CONTINUED:

PANEL TWO: Walking nervously through a grove of trees in Bachelors Grove Cemetery, SALLY hugs herself, shivering in the cold rain that begins to fall. The girl remains unaware that the ghostly MADONNA watches her as the specter sits on a headstone while the House recedes towards the horizon.

> **6 CAPTION/OMNI**: Her mind raced. Moving forward meant safety, but at the cost of her mother's continual lecturing.

> **7 SALLY** (THOT): Oh, great. RAIN! How did I get HERE? My head hurts. Was I DRUGGED? My clothes are RUINED.

PANEL THREE: SALLY looks about nervously, her cell phone in her hand, unaware of the man watching her from behind a tree (RON FITZGERALD – reference available). He is cloaked in shadows, almost a silhouette. However, we can see the moonlight reflecting from the ornate stitching in his jacket as well as his eyes, the right one of which is totally white, seemingly dead.

> **8 CAPTION/OMNI**: She glanced back to see no house, only darkness and grave markers. Staying HERE was no sane option.

> **9 SALLY** (THOT): Can I even get a SIGNAL in this place? Who would I CALL anyway? I have no real friends. Certainly not those grabby CREEPS at the party.

PAGE TWO (6 PANELS)

PANEL ONE: SALLY whirls around, but not in Ron's off-panel direction. From her body language, she is definitely poised for fight or flight.

> **1 CAPTION/OMNI**: In a cemetery, EVERY noise is a potential WARNING, especially if you're TERRIFIED.

> **2 SALLY**: WHO IS IT?

PANEL TWO: THADDEUS PITT (appears in his mid-30s, dark brown hair and beard, see model sheet) leans against a tree. His arms are crossed, and his smile is gentle, his gaze seductive, as he looks at SALLY whose head is cocked in his direction. She's more intrigued than frightened.

> **3 PITT**: I'm so sorry. I'm THADDEUS PITT. I forgot just how FRIGHTENING this place can be, especially to a beautiful young lady such as yourself.

> **4 SALLY**: *gasp* Th-that's okay. Who says I'm scared?

CONTINUED:

PAGE TWO CONTINUED:

PANEL THREE: PITT emerges from his place of concealment and SALLY is clearly thrilled as she takes in the sight of this handsome man.

> **5 PITT**: Then I apologize for startling you. I can hear your heart beating deliciously from here. And your name?

> **6 SALLY**: *cough* I'm Sal – um, TABATHA DARQUE … nice to meet you … handsome.

PANEL FOUR: With a sly smile, PITT moves his hand through SALLY's hair as his mouth nears her neck. Her eyes are closed and she's clearly seduced.

> **7 PITT**: I smell your delicious FRUSTRATION, Tabitha. You crave more … EXPERIENCED seductions, do you not?

> **8 SALLY**: Oooh, yessss … I've always liked older guys, no offense … they're smoother, more polite …

PANEL FIVE: SALLY's eyes are closed as she awaits PITT's kiss on her neck. However, the man reveals his dangerous fangs that are ready to pierce the tender flesh of her throat.

> **9 PITT**: The anticipation … a kiss on the neck … the unbearably delicious suspense …

> **10 PITT**: And then PENETRATION.

PAGE THREE (5 PANELS)

PANEL ONE: On SALLY's near-orgasmic expression as PITT sinks his fangs deep into the side of her throat. A small trickle of blood moves down her neck and she drops her phone.

> **1 SALLY** (THOT): OOOH! I've always heard how GOOD this would feel ... getting light headed ...

> **2 SALLY** (THOT): The other girls will be so jealous ... should I tell him I'm only 17?

PANEL TWO: SALLY's eyes go wide with panic while PITT's fangs draw even more blood that now stains her clothing and flows down her shoulder.

> **3 SALLY** (THOT) Oh, wait ... blood on my dress ... feel so cold ... am I dying ...

> **4 SALLY** (THOT): I'M DYING! OH GOD! WHY CAN'T I SCREAM???

> **5 RON** (O.P.): LET HER <u>GO</u>!

CONTINUED:

PAGE THREE CONTINUED:

PANEL THREE: RON FITZGERALD enters the panel, although we can't see his face yet, just as PITT lowers SALLY's limp, nearly-dead body to the cemetery grounds. Sally's soul begins to rise from her body.

> **6 RON**: CRAP! I was too SLOW! The girl better be ALL RIGHT or –

> **7 PITT** (SPOOKY): Or WHAT, failed WIZARD? Your DARK STICKY powers have let you down once again, RON FITZGERALD.

> **8 SALLY** (THOT): Feel weightless ... free of my cares ... no friends ... I'm floating ... floating ...

PANEL FOUR: RON FITZGERALD, still mostly off-panel, points towards off-panel. SALLY's spirit turns in that direction, terror and confusion on her face. NOTE: a glowing chain, her chakra, runs from her soul's midsection to that of her former body.

> **9 RON**: LISTEN, girl! LEAVE this place! SAVE YOURSELF!

> **10 SALLY** (GHOSTLY): Who are you? How can you see me? What about your EYE?

> **11 RON**: NEVER MIND how I can see you. RUN!

> **12 SOUND FX** (O.P. DEMONS): GRRRLLWWWW! HHSSSS!

CONTINUED:

PAGE THREE CONTINUED:

PANEL FIVE: A flock of hideous DEMONS race towards a panic-stricken SALLY as she tries to fly away, but she finds herself anchored to her physical body by her chakra and it's wrapped around her ankles

13 **SALLY** (GHOSTLY): DEMONS? WHAT do they WANT? I have NOTHING left.

14 **RON** (O.P.): The LAST thing this HELLPACK wants is your SOUL. Their DESTINATION is far more USEFUL to them.

PAGE FOUR (5 PANELS)

PANEL ONE: SALLY reacts in horror as her hand passes through her body while the DEMONS are almost on her ghostly self.

> **1 SALLY** (GHOSTLY): Oh, GOD! Am I a GHOST?

> **2 RON** (O.P.): You THINK? Better to be DISEMBODIED than what THEY plan for you.

PANEL TWO: PITT strangles SALLY with her own chakra, pulling her away from her physical body as the DEMONS gleefully tear at it, molest it, sink their talons into it.

> **3 PITT** (SPOOKY): Tasty virgin soul, you are now one of the DAMNED! I claim you as MY OWN!

> **4 SALLY** (GHOSTLY): No – this is happening too fast – someone – SAVE ME!

PANEL THREE: AZTEROKK, a buff demon with fangs that drip venom, seizes SALLY's physical body's, wrenching the mouth open as RON watches helplessly, DEMONS clutching him, slicing his flesh with their talons. Other DEMONS attack the Muscle Demon as well as Sally's body.

> **5 AZTEROKK** (SPOOKY): BACK, you pieces of OFFAL! I have waited since THE GREAT FLOOD for a body like THIS.

CONTINUED:

PAGE FOUR CONTINUED:

> **6 RON**: LEAVE her BE, AZTEROKK! HELL will hold NO terrors once I get ahold of you!

PANEL FOUR: Clutching helplessly at the chakra with which PITT strangles her, SALLY cries as she watches AZTEROKK wriggle into her body as if putting on a pair of too-tight overalls. The demon's back is to her.

> **8 AZTEROKK** (SPOOKY): *unph* Empty WORDS, as ALWAYS, my HALF-SIGHTED MAGI. *ukk* I didn't think she'd be THIS tight for me.

> **7 SALLY** (GHOSTLY): What are you DOING to me? I'm not made of SPANDEX!

> **8 AZTEROKK** (SPOOKY): Be SILENT, little slut-to-be –

PANEL FIVE: On AZTEROKK, now in Sally's body, as he/she twists around to face the off-panel girl. The body's expression is gleefully cruel, and "she" stands like a coiled spring, ready to attack. There are bloody scars around her mouth from where the skin was stretched and torn as the chakra falls away from Sally's astral ankles.

> **9 AZTEROKK** (SPOOKY): – and HANG ON TIGHT!

> **10 AZTEROKK** (SPOOKY, SHOUT): Your stroll through HELL has just BEGUN!

PAGE FIVE (6 PANELS)

PANEL ONE: AZTEROKK grins as he runs his hands appreciatively over Sally's body while SALLY watches fearfully, powerless to stop him as PITT holds tight with a leer. The physical body begins to lose some of the gashes from the demons and from Azterokk's invasion.

> **1 AZTEROKK** (SPOOKY): Warm blood again … untested flesh … what JOY to have such an unsullied virgin shell again.

> **2 AZTEROKK** (SPOOKY): Oh, stop WEEPING, human infant. AZTEROKK intends to give you a gift –

PANEL TWO: AZTEROKK pushes the free end of the chakra into "his" navel, pulling SALLY helplessly along for the ride.

> **3 AZTEROKK** (SPOOKY, SHOUT): – THE BEST SEAT IN THE HOUSE!

> **4 SALLY** (GHOSTLY): EEEEEEEEK! PLEASE GIVE ME BACK MY BODY!

PANEL THREE: SALLY pulls desperately at the chakra, much to a leering AZTEROKK's delight. In the background, RON FITZGERALD shrugs off the DEMONS flaying his skin.

CONTINUED:

PAGE FIVE CONTINUED:

5 SALLY (GHOSTLY): PLEASE let me GO!

6 AZTEROKK (SPOOKY): Your TERROR is DELECTIBLE, girl. You are a FEAST of FEAR.

7 RON: RELEASE HER or find out why I'm called MASTER Ron Fitzgerald!

PANEL FOUR: RON FITZGERALD pulls out a crucifix and holds it in front of AZTEROKK who recoils from the sight. There is a little smoke issuing from where Ron holds the cross.

8 RON: In the name of THE CREATOR, go back to HELL so the girl's spirit can find PEACE. I COMMAND IT!

9 AZTEROKK (SPOOKY): You have no right to – AGKKK! The hated icon BURNS this form!

10 POLICE (ELECTRONIC, O.P.): Hold it right there.

CONTINUED:

PAGE FIVE CONTINUED:

PANEL FIVE: Both AZTEROKK, who still recoils from Ron's off-panel attack, and PITT are distracted by a red light shining from something else off-panel, but in the other direction.

> **11 AZTEROKK** (SPOOKY): WHAT? POLICE? What a tasty DESSERT.

> **12 PITT** (SPOOKY): NO! RUN! You aren't yet fully bonded to your body. Take the virgin to our LAIR. I'll cover your tracks.

PANEL SIX: SALLY turns in response to an off-panel voice as AZTEROKK leaps over the headstones, dragging the girl's spirit by her chakra.

> **13 VOICES** (DISEMBODIED BALLOON, ALSO GHOSTLY): Do not fight … have no fear … all will be explained … just go along …

> **14 SALLY** (GHOSTLY, THOT): Voices … soothing … warm … too scared to fight anyway …

PAGE SIX (5 PANELS)

PANEL ONE: Two uniformed POLICEMEN arrive on the scene, their flashlights barely missing the various fleeing DEMONS and PITT who leaps into the thick of the trees.

> **1 1st POLICEMAN**: All of you FREEZE! I said – HEY, where'd they GO?

> **2 2nd POLICEMAN**: Aw, don't waste your breath. These KIDS never listen. Hey, is that –?

PANEL TWO: The two POLICEMEN frame RON FITZGERALD in the glare of their flashlights. Ron shields his eyes from the light, but his right eye seems to stand out against the shadows.

> **3 1st POLICEMAN**: Oh, YOU again! So what brings you to Bachelors Grove THIS time, Fitzgerald?

> **4 RON**: The usual, officer … the dream that burns in my head.

> **5 1st POLICEMAN**: Okay, pal. Let's take the rest of the night off.

CONTINUED:

PAGE SIX CONTINUED:

PANEL THREE: PITT and AZTEROKK land in front of a crypt where two other vampires, LUTHER ROBERTS (male, young, glasses, sweater vest & bow tie, reference available) and ANTOINE D'LACEY (male, black, casual dress, reference available) look up.

> **6 CAPTION/1ST POLICEMAN**: "I think the excitement's over for one night."

> **7 PITT** (SPOOKY): Home again, home again.

> **8 D'LACEY** (SPOOKY): About damn time. I see we have a new … CUTE friend.

PANEL FOUR: ROBERTS and D'LACEY crouch, ready to attack, their fangs bared, and their expressions twisted into cruel, vile, sneers. But PITT stands between them and AZTEROKK who in turn, stands ready for a fight.

> **9 ROBERTS** (SPOOKY): Fresh blood! Warm MEAT! HSSSSS!

> **10 PITT** (SPOOKY): STAND DOWN. She's one of us now.

> **11 CAPTION/SALLY**: "No! No, I'm NOT!"

> > **CONTINUED**:

PAGE SIX CONTINUED:

PANEL FIVE: Tethered above AZTEROKK, SALLY's body language mimics her host body's as it straightens up, the potential conflict defusing.

   12 SALLY (GHOSTLY): That MAGICIAN saw me. Why can't anyone else?

   13 IMON (GHOSTLY, O.P.): WE can see you.

PAGE SEVEN (5 PANELS)

PANEL ONE: ROBERTS, D'LACEY, and PITT face AZTEROKK, all with fangs bared and appearing more like monsters than humans. Above them hover their more innocent-looking counterparts (in order) IMON OSTHOFT (male, ancient Egyptian, slender, wise eyes, reference available), GARY ABELARD (male, glasses, bow tie, reference available), and THOMAS WAYHILL (male, reference available), including a surprised SALLY.

    1 ROBERTS (SPOOKY): Welcome to our CABAL, Missy. Ready for the bloody HUNT?

    2 IMON (GHOSTLY): Please listen, young lady. Allow us to help you.

    3 SALLY (GHOSTLY): H-how can you help me? What's happening? Who are you?

PANEL TWO: More on IMON, GARY, and THOMAS than their vampiric counterparts as they speak to SALLY. All three men are smiling – Imon smiles wisely through thin lips, Gary gives the peace sign, and Thomas places his hand on his chest and bows slightly.

    4 IMON (GHOSTLY): Allow me to introduce ourselves. I am IMON OSTHOFT and these are my friends, GARY ABELARD and THOMAS WAYHILL.

                                      CONTINUED:

PAGE SEVEN CONTINUED:

    5 THOMAS (GHOSTLY): It's our pleasure, Miss …?

    6 SALLY (GHOSTLY): Sally … oh, no … I can hear this demon's THOUGHTS … what he wants to do … I can't stop LISTENING. Am I in HELL? MOMMY!!!

PANEL THREE: THOMAS takes SALLY's ghostly hand in both of his.

    7 THOMAS (GHOSTLY): No, we think of it more as PURGATORY, if you must know. It's not much comfort, I know.

    8 SALLY (GHOSTLY): That hideous demon is reading my own MEMORIES … I feel so … so VIOLATED.

PANEL FOUR: SALLY stares into her palms as IMON smiles benevolently at her.

    9 SALLY (GHOSTLY): I can hear this … VAMPIRE'S thoughts … if my body does HALF of what's passing through … MY mind … I want to VOMIT … but I can't …

    10 IMON (GHOSTLY): I can see your soul is troubled, but UNSULLIED. What your PHYSICAL FORM does will not affect your entry into PARADISE.

                CONTINUED:

PAGE SEVEN CONTINUED:

PANEL FIVE: THOMAS looks down with dark concern at PITT who rubs his hands together in anticipatory delight.

> **11 THOMAS** (GHOSTLY): Your soul is safe while you RESIST. Just don't start ENJOYING what your host body does. I've seen too many that gave in to the darkness, lost for ETERNITY.

> **12 PITT** (SPOOKY): The hunt ... snap the humans' bones ... suck their sweet MARROW for hours ... then maybe allow them to DIE only when we grow BORED.

PAGE EIGHT (4 PANELS)

PANEL ONE: THOMAS reaches towards SALLY who tugs futilely at her chakra which now glows reddish-gold.

> **1 THOMAS** (GHOSTLY): No, Sally. You mustn't shatter the CHAKRA which BINDS you to your CAPTOR. Even if it was POSSIBLE, your soul would dissipate painfully. Best to leave it be.

> **2 SALLY** (GHOSTLY): But I can't stay tethered to this MONSTER. I just want to go HOME.

PANEL TWO: SALLY's jaw drops as IMON points to GARY and THOMAS.

> **3 IMON** (GHOSTLY): You must be patient, just like us.

> **4 SALLY** (GHOSTLY): I don't know if I can.

> **5 THOMAS** (GHOSTLY): You can … you MUST … once you learn what WE know.

PANEL THREE: ROBERTS growls at D'LACEY as above them in spirit form, IMON places a gentle hand on ABELARD's shoulder as they look at an off-panel Sally.

> **6 IMON** (GHOSTLY): Poor girl. I fear she might go mad … give in to her horror, just like too many I've seen over the centuries.

CONTINUED:

PAGE EIGHT CONTINUED:

7 ABELARD (GHOSTLY): No … we can't let her. We can SAVE this one. Let her know our SECRET.

8 ROBERTS (SPOOKY): Find the warmbloods and tear them open for their still-beating hearts – EAT their GUTS while they WATCH.

9 D'LACEY (SPOOKY): Yes, wait for them to enter this accursed place before we PLAY with our FOOD.

PANEL FOUR: SALLY leans forward, weeping into her hands as THOMAS tries to reach over and hold her, just falling short of success. Below them, tied by their chakras, are AZTEROKK, luxuriating in his new power and body, with PITT.

10 SALLY: I just want to see my MOM … my HOME … go back to SCHOOL … why does my mouth taste like BLOOD? I hear its THOUGHTS … rape … murder … torture … *sob*

11 THOMAS(GHOSTLY): It'll get WORSE before it gets BETTER … but can I tell you a SECRET?

12 AZTEROKK (SPOOKY): This is LIFE? This blood is TURGID … ICY … I thirst for TERROR …

13 PITT (SPOOKY): Rush out NOW and you're beyond our HELP! Our FOES are many and you are IGNORANT of your true POTENTIAL … but can I tell you a SECRET?

PAGE NINE (5 PANELS)

PANEL ONE: In the foreground of the panel, the crucifix lies stuck in the dirt as the TWO POLICEMEN lead RON FITZGERALD towards a squad car.

 1 CAPTION/PITT: "Our prey does not believe we EXIST. And our TORMENTORS are FEW, OVERCONFIDENT and FINITE. There are more of us than they realize and we have all ETERNITY to FEAST on their VITALS."

 2 CAPTION/PITT: "The advantages of TIME and POWER belong to US!"

PANEL TWO: AZTEROKK moves towards a crypt on the cemetery grounds, towing SALLY behind him via the chakra. PITT stands at the crypt door, ushering his ally inside.

 3 CAPTION/SALLY: "Guys? I can barely HEAR you. Please don't leave me. What SECRET?"

 4 PITT (SPOOKY): INSIDE! The sunrise nears.

 5 CAPTION/IMON: "This is IMON speaking… this secret has kept us SANE for … well, Gary is a mere 63 years old, Thomas is only 287, and I haven't seen a SUNRISE in well over 3,000 YEARS."

PANEL THREE: A would-be VAMPIRE HUNTER (physical description available), stake and mallet in her hands, eyes the crypt from behind a withered tree as the sunrise covers the cemetery and the woman in a warm red glow.

CONTINUED:

PAGE NINE CONTINUED:

> **6 CAPTION/SALLY**: "What are you saying? That's INSANE!"

> **7 CAPTION/IMON**: "And being one of the FEASTING UNDEAD isn't? There is much you have yet to learn, young friend."

PANEL FOUR: AZTEROKK curls up into a ball inside the casket he's just torn open. The decomposed BODY of the coffin's previous occupant lies on the cold stone floor.

> **8 CAPTION/SALLY**: "So what is this SECRET that will keep me SANE while my BODY commits all these CRIMES?

> **9 CAPTION/IMON**: "Our secret speaks to us in our waking dreams, gives us succor in our PERGATORY …

PANEL FIVE: An ANGEL with a flaming sword held aloft dispels the night's shadows of the cemetery. He stands strong, confident as the ghostly MADONNA watches impassively from behind standing beside the HOUSE with the POND in one corner.

> **10 CAPTION/IMON**: "We have a hidden CHAMPION who will RESCUE us one day. Thus, our SECRET SALVATION is that we have …

CONTINUED:

PAGE NINE CONTINUED:

11 TITLE (MATCHING THE STYLE OF THE TITLE ON PAGE ONE): HOPE!

12 CAPTION/OMNI: And this is but ONE of the many

13 LOGO: TALES OF BACHELORS GROVE

14 CAPTION/OMNI: We look forward to telling you the OTHERS … BRACE YOURSELF!

15 CREDITS: STORY/INSPIRATION: CHARLES D. MOISANT – SCRIPT/PLOT ASSIST: BRIAN K. MORRIS – ART: TBD – LETTERS: TBD – COLORS: TBD – EDITING: CHARLES D. MOISANT

Chapter Six - The Comic Book Unleashed

With "We Have …" selected as the first issue's lead, Charles and I worked with writer/artist Mike Reidy on his thriller, "Run, Hide, Die," a story co-plotted with Charles D. Moisant. Mike and I butted heads several times over the course of editing the script (I wrote an early draft and eventually removed my name once most of the elements I added were omitted in Mike's rewrite), but we ended up respecting each other, which was good. And we agreed to disagree, which was also more than acceptable. But Mike is a fabulous talent and I was tickled to see the finished product.

Then I was proud as could be when my dear friend and personal inspiration, Paul Barile, got his very first comic book script published, "A Kiss In the Night," with art from a gentleman that Charles and I met at The Porter County Monster Con in Valparaiso, Indiana. Jorge Garza handled not just the moody artwork, but the lettering and coloring too. When Paul saw the finished comic book for the first time, I believe tears of joy welled up in his eyes. This won't be the last time you see either of these men's work in a Silver Phoenix title.

With my text story and the spine-tingling Pui Che cover, we had a comic book. Charles and I ran a brief Kickstarter campaign to defray some of the production expenses. It proved to be a LOT of hard work, but we ended up with around $3,300, or 110% of our goal.

This book was one of the incentives, so you have our Kickstarter supporters to thank.

So once the comic was laid out and sent to the printer, Charles executed a short run of the issue, just to test the sales waters at The Spook Show horror convention in Mattoon, Illinois. We hoped people would be interested and want the comic.

We sold out in three days.

Next, Charles printed up a LOT of copies from which we'd sign and send out to our Kickstarter supporters. It's generated a LOT of compliments at shows so we're confident in starting production on future issues.

Chapter Seven - Stories in Text

The idea of the comic book text story originated in the late 1930s. Many comic publishers sold their comics via mail subscriptions. However, to gain the coveted 4th Class Mailing Permit that made this practice economically feasible, magazines were required to print at least two pages of text in every issue.

Many early comics published prose tales of their comic characters while others created informational pieces, presumably to counter parental allegations concerning the non-educational aspects of the medium. In time, these pages gave way to letter columns where readers would comment on the contents of earlier issues.

When brainstorming the contents of *THTOBG* #1, Charles expressed a desire to run a text story. It just so happened I wanted the challenge of writing a really, really short story with real characters, conflict, and a satisfying ending. So, I came up with "Cool Seductions" to showcase the Pond. Future installments would spotlight a different aspect of the cemetery.

To intrigue Charles, I came up with a logline:

A woman decides to seduce the Devil in exchange for Lucifer's favor. But the pond is a jealous woman who takes her sacrifices seriously.

I also wanted to establish the Pond's sentience and the notion that although some participants in these stories could "hear" and comprehend the waters' many moods, the reader never would.

Charles also counted the number of words in a couple of old text stories and so 1,500 (more or less) was my word count. Here is the result:

COOL SEDUCTIONS

(Originally published in *The Haunting Tales of Bachelors Grove* #1, 2017)

She was fluid. She could never see herself anywhere but in Bachelors Grove with its often-dangerous winters and stifling summers. She waxed and waned with the elements, drawing strength from the land that surrounded her and fortified by the cool Illinois rains.

Her life's blood nurtured the Cemetery, transforming its lush plant life from the browns and oranges and crimsons of Autumn into the verdure of Summer. Being female, the cemetery constantly complained that it was too full, that the finite mortals who trod its lands were careless and disrespectful to one so old and bloated with corrupted flesh.

By way of reply, she smiled softly in her way, nodded gently like the waves that covered her surface during the breezes of Spring, and went about her way.

She was the pond, the nameless body of water whose slender fingers wove through the underground tapestry of Bachelors Grove Cemetery.

Dozens of people wandered through Bachelors Grove every week. Some came to mourn. Others indulged their fantasies or fed their superstitions amidst the mature greenery, moss-covered headstones, and winding foot paths.

A visitor arrived one frosty sundown in November. Skarlett Rage's raven hair perfectly matched her tight leather trousers and form-gripping halter. She exited a building made of sorcery and judgment, one that fled into the distance as her steel-hard gaze raked its ancient timbers. Once it faded from her view, the woman shrugged and strolled towards the pond. Skarlett stood on the banks of the pond and tried to see to its floor.

"You can almost count the bodies, can't you?"

Another woman might have gasped when a steady baritone voice broke the silence. But Skarlett turned casually and greeted the visitor with a gentle smile. "Greetings, Lord Lucifer."

The man before her was dressed immaculately from the polish of his jet-black shoes, upwards along the lines of his pleated trousers, to the form-fitting – but in no way constraining – cut of his ebony jacket with matching shirt and necktie, all of the purest silks. His hair flowed freely from the widow's peak at the apex of his unlined forehead onto his shoulders. The man's smile pulled softly at the corners of his mouth, refusing to commit to a full grin.

"Pleased to meet you," Lucifer stated without warmth. "Glad you guessed my name."

She pressed a black fingernail against her chin, smiled broadly, then executed an exaggerated curtsy. "Clever as always, milord."

"And impatient." The edge in Lucifer's voice could perform surgery. Then the fallen angel laughed heartily. "If this is about your mortal soul, I've owned that particular commodity for years. You are wagering with funds you lost long ago, and I don't provide loans." His expression turned dark. "I would listen to your offer, however. Amuse me."

"I offer sacrifice, Lord Lucifer." Skarlett gestured towards the pond. "This water holds perhaps hundreds of bodies, many of whom were innocents taken before they could repent their sins. I would use my earthly charms to lure more here, to play upon their lusts, and then snuff them out until the banks of this water overflow. All in your service, of course."

Lucifer nodded thoughtfully. "Well, that's all well and good. But I already have someone here who will extinguish the divine spark and leave their bodies to rot."

The woman's eyes flared in response to the unspoken challenge. "Then I propose that I do it for the fun of the act."

Skarlett drew her breath in deeply. "And you can keep my soul. Just think of me mercifully when the Final Event arrives, and you are forced into your infernal kingdom for all of time."

Darkness gathered around the fallen angel's eyes. "You gamble that after all these millennia, I recall how to feel anything that resembles gratitude or mercy."

"Then call it an appeal to your sense of bemusement." She turned her head from left to right and back again before she located her prey. "Watch this and then decide." With that command, Skarlett walked with purpose towards a freshly-dug grave and the man standing beside it.

He wore a tweed suit from his father that just happened to fit his portly frame. The man couldn't sew the patches over his elbows without drawing blood. However, the only person who knew how now lay under the loosely-packed soil.   He wept for this and many other losses.

"Lonely?" Skarlett asked. She smiled as his eyes roamed down and then up her shapely form, stopping last at her dark-rimmed eyes. She saw a bit of "Why me?" in his gaze, but the man's nervous blinking told the same story she'd read in every straight male's gaze since she became a teenager. That story always concluded the same way because she'd learned how to write the ending.

Turning towards the pond, Lucifer smiled. "Jealous? You might have competition."

The pond rippled gently and emitted what sounded like a gurgle.

"Oh, I know," Lucifer whispered. "You sacrifice unwillingly, like so many of your gender." He nodded towards Skarlett and her prey. "Let's watch, shall we?"

Unable to remove his eyes from the dark vision before him, the man at the graveside forgot about his late wife and their respectable friends. Sweat beaded cold around his retreating hairline.

Skarlett smiled with confidence as she edged towards the man's face, her lips pursed and ready to meet his. She took one of his chins between her perfectly-sculpted fingernails in the hopes of controlling his quivering. His heart beat so wildly that she could almost hear it.

As Skarlett's lips neared her target, she withdrew a hypodermic from the waistband of her skirt. As she had done so many times before, she would slide the needle into her victim's flesh and inject the clear fluid that would paralyze the man's body while sharpening his wits and senses, leaving him fully conscious and aware of the indignities done to him.

She first used the vile formula to liberate her victims from the burden of carrying their wallets on a dare from her first boyfriend until she seduced the recipe from him. The next morning, he awakened in a bathtub full of ice while she woke up in a suite at the Plaza.

The tip of the needle hovered, ready to violate the man's pasty flesh. He smelled the clove on her breath and felt the heat of her flawless skin. Skarlett savored the moment before the strike, that feeling of total control, a feeling she'd never known until she'd run away from home for the Windy City.

A heartbeat before the thin steel tube could pierce her victim's skin, cold washed over Skarlett's body, violently stealing her breath. A bubbling filled her ears and when her senses returned, she heard her intended victim scream like a schoolgirl before racing off in the other direction.

Skarlett surveyed her leather and nylon-clad body. Stagnant water invaded her clothing, icy fingers sliding against her cooling flesh and blurring the sharp lines of her makeup. The night air slapped her in frigid waves like a mother disciplining a wayward child. Skarlett turned towards the fallen angel, her eyes wide with astonishment and thought processes so jumbled, she couldn't form her first question to her lord and owner.

Lucifer smiled admiringly at the pond. Pieces of old plant life and decayed bones rested on its now-placid surface before disappearing once again into its cobalt depths.

"This lady is older than you can imagine," Lucifer explained patiently, "and her motives are hers alone, never for us to decipher." He sighed. "But she is jealous, often ravenous, and takes challenge poorly."

Attempting to pull her dangerously-long heels from the muddy grounds, Skarlett screamed at Lucifer. "I don't know what kind of crap is going on, but I didn't summon you here to –"

"*You* summoned *me*?" Genuine anger flashed in the dark lord's eyes. "I am on *no* being's leash." He didn't even glance at the pond as he whispered, "She is yours."

Skarlett wanted to plead for another chance, to offer her beauty and guile to Lucifer's service. However, water now filled her mouth and lungs as she clawed against the icy liquid that sapped her strength.

Panic filled Skarlett's mind. Desperately, she silently

prayed to Lucifer and to all the gods she no longer believed in for just one more breath. As the last of her strength left her, the woman felt her body rest atop a dark altar comprised of rotten flesh from generations past before she felt nothing more.

At the water's edge, Lucifer softly applauded. "Well played, milady." A grin split his perfect profile as he took a step back into an envelope of flame.

"Like my creator," Lucifer stated, "you work in mysterious ways." He added without a trace of charm, "I shall see you again soon, milady," before vanishing from Bachelors Grove, leaving nothing behind but the stench of brimstone and regret.

THE END

And some stories cannot be contained in a mere 1,500 words.

Some stories cannot be done justice in the comics format.

Some stories of obsession must be told more fully.

WHERE IS DAPHNE? WHERE IS DAPHNE?

by

Brian K. Morris

Fresh out of college, this girl, yours truly, used all the influence of a not-too-hard-earned Liberal Arts degree to snag a job as a second shift telemarketer. The gig was easy to score and slightly less demeaning than swinging from a silver pole, attracting well-creased dollar bills and hastily-scribbled phone numbers.

It was good to have another career option, or so I told my mother who constantly complained about my lack of ambition. If I had no ambition at all, I wouldn't be picking up a half-shift from a buddy who wanted a night off, right?

On the other hand, telemarketing paid far less than stripping. I constantly lived from paycheck to almost-the-next paycheck.

While the sun edged towards the horizon, I pressed the accelerator to the extreme limits of my courage as I approached Bachelors Grove Park on my right. I believed I could clear the evening traffic, clock in without getting docked a half hour's pay, and then figure out when I could

149

remove my jacket before hitting the call lists.

Perhaps I should have paid more attention to my surroundings than my plans to outwit that fascist I called a supervisor.

From my left, I caught a flash of white just before my Subaru connected hard with someone sprinting across the four-lane highway and center turn lane. A slender woman flew into the air, landing a dozen feet in front of where my car struck her. I brought the car to a screeching halt a couple of seconds before the person stopped rolling across the asphalt, her limbs splayed at terrifying angles.

Pain tore through my chest as the body came to a stop. I wondered if I'd killed a person and immediately felt the need to vomit, to cry, to drive off, to scream, to hyperventilate. Relief swept over me when I saw no blood on the pale mini-dress she wore. No blood, no death, I reasoned.

Framed in the crossbeam of my headlights, I exited my car and sprinted towards the unmoving victim of my carelessness. Not surprisingly, no other car stopped to help me, although a few slowed down to gawk. When I tried to meet the passengers' eyes, to motion for help, they turned away and accelerated into the lengthening shadows of evening.

I knelt beside the girl. She couldn't have graduated from high school yet. Her pale clothing showed traces of large polka dots, calf-clinging boots, a wide vinyl belt, and a skirt so short that defending her modesty would be impossible. Her light brown bangs just touched the edges of her eyebrows.

As I fumbled for my phone, desperately rehearsing the account I intended to give the authorities, the girl suddenly opened her eyes, her gaze locked with mine.

"Where is Daphne?" she whispered fearfully. Then she repeated herself with a deafening scream, "*Where is Daphne?*"

The phone fell from my grasp, landing on the wide vinyl belt that ran across her narrow midriff. I fought the urge to leap to my feet and flee. However, even if I was coward enough to risk a police charge for leaving the scene of a crime, the woman's fingers dug deep into my forearms like nails in a two-by-four. I couldn't move if I tried.

"Please," I whimpered, "I need to call you an ambulance. God, I'm so sorry for what happened. Let me −"

The woman's eyes raked the highway frantically. "Where is Daphne? Where is Daphne?"

I finally slipped my arm free of the girl's grasp to retrieve my phone. Pain from her tourniquet-like grip, as well as the tingle of blood re-entering that arm, distracted me as I dialed 911. I noted, with some relief, that this woman's nails left white marks on my flesh, but drew no blood, just as the operator picked up the line.

"Nine-one-one," the male dispatcher's voice stated professionally. "What is the nature of your emergency."

"Oh, God! I accidentally hit a girl. I didn't mean to." My eyes stung from the tears I hoped wouldn't fall. I wanted to be so grown-up at that moment, hoping I wouldn't be charged with Attempted Vehicular Manslaughter. "I'm on one-forty-third, east of Ridgeland, I think." I looked around for an address number for all the good it did me. "There's a big parking lot on the – oh what is it? – the north side of the highway; big electrical converter on the opposite side. Wow, can't you ping me or something?"

"Ma'am, please keep calm." If only I could be as cool as the guy on the other end of our conversation. "Are you in need of medical assistance?"

"No, no, I'm fine," And I was, if you ignored the fact that this crazy lady just tried to pull my arm off. "But I hit someone with my car. T-there's no blood, but I think she hit her head." I glanced down at her again. Her wild eyes radiated almost feral anger, fueled by a palpable frustration with her inability to locate this Daphne, whoever she was. Trying to be helpful to the dispatcher, I added, "This woman is young, long brown hair, keeps asking for a 'Daphne.'"

"Daphne?" The line went quiet for a second before he asked slowly, "Ma'am, this is important. Did you say 'Daphne?'"

Frightened and impatient to be gone, I almost yelled, "Yes, that's what I said. Da–" The name halted in my throat as I looked down at the pavement.

No one lay there.

The dispatcher's voice pulled me from my confused state. "Miss? Are you still there?"

I stated numbly, "Um, she appears to have … um, gone." For a moment, I almost chuckled at the notion of using the words *appears* and *vanished* in the same sentence. I wondered if I was going into shock. "D-did you get my location?"

The dispatcher's professional demeanor returned. "I know exactly where you are, Ma'am. You should be hearing a squad car in just a few seconds, and an ambulance is on its way with an E.T.A. of three minutes."

I rose to my feet. I saw no footprints in the grass beyond the nearby curb, no sign of the girl's exit nor any evidence that she'd been there in the first place. *Where did you go, lady?*

Running down the list of possibilities for this insane incident, a quick glance at the cracked plastic on my bumper, told me this situation was more than a delusion.

A siren arrived from the west, its mechanical wail seizing my attention. My head turned towards the approaching police car and its hypnotically-strobing blue and red lights. I spun back around, still looking for the woman, worried that she might have internal bleeding, broken some ribs, received a concussion, or might be dying just beyond my view.

"But – but she's gone," I confessed to the dispatcher.

"That's okay," the dispatcher stated calmly. "The ambulance is for you, not her."

The eastward-pointing Midlothian Police car braked opposite me before turning on its lights, compelling all vehicular traffic to stop in both directions. Cutting across the westbound lanes, the black-and-white came to a screeching stop behind my car. I noticed I'd turned on my emergency blinkers automatically as I left my vehicle. *Hooray for being responsible.*

I watched the policeman speak into his handheld microphone from behind the driver's wheel. From all the crime dramas I'd seen on television, I assumed my plates were being run. Immediately, my gut burned as I recalled my unpaid parking tickets, but couldn't remember just how many I'd stuffed into my glove compartment, promising myself I'd pay them eventually.

The officer exited his vehicle, the blue and red lights flashing wildly enough to stimulate a seizure. As he walked alongside his car, his face took on an almost demonic aspect as the crimson and cyan beams played across his handsome features.

I stood up, feeling like my first-grade principal caught me trying to sneak out of class again. The officer's cap covered what appeared to be close-cropped brown hair, and his body fat percentage had to have been in the single digits. While his face held few of what might be called distinguishing features, the only aspect that might put me off would have been his completely neutral expression. Otherwise, under less stressful circumstances, I might have hoped he'd ask me out.

"Hello there," the policeman said without an ounce of accusation in his voice, which surprised me. In fact, he seemed to take the possibility of someone dying all in stride, unless that's how the cops were supposed to handle us these days, all calm and collected until I slipped and revealed where I stashed the body.

"Would you please turn off your engine?" the officer asked. I immediately complied, going as far as to pull my keys from the ignition and place them on the dashboard. Then I placed my hands on the steering wheel, keeping them in plain sight, while debating with myself whether smiling the him would be either considered polite or too macabre, considering what I just did.

Then he asked, "Do you have your driver's license, registration, and insurance card on you?" He cast a quick glance at the front of my car and the remnants of my once-intact bumper.

I tried not to stutter. "It's in my purse on the front seat. Can I get it?" I added, "You can if you want. If it'll make you feel safer, sir." I read once that a traffic stop was the most dangerous part of police work, that they approached most vehicles in a state of justifiable wariness. I sure didn't want this guy thinking I carried a Glock in my handbag.

Although the lights from his car still created unearthly shadows on the officer's face, his voice softened. "No, that's okay. You grab the cards and meet me back in the car when the EMTs are done with you." With that, he returned to his vehicle to study his laptop computer. I opened my door and grabbed my purse from the passenger's seat. I waited for the ambulance to pull up, which it did one minute later than the dispatcher promised.

A quick series of questions and on-site tests later, the medic left me with an admonition to visit my doctor as soon as possible, maybe even treat myself to an x-ray. Once the ambulance moved back into the flow of traffic, I walked quickly to the squad car, my handbag held out before me in plain sight.

"Let me clear some room for you." The officer swept an insulated lunchbox onto the floor of the passenger's side of the squad car. I entered and realized I didn't look at the officer's name tag. Leaning forward to see my interrogator's identity, I found the laptop blocked my view. Not wanting to appear as if I was taking his name to file a complaint, I sat back and kept silent.

He studied his screen and without looking up, he asked,

"So, you saw Naomi?" Instead of speaking, I gasped. He added, "Brown hair, bangs, boots, looks like she escaped one of those TV dance shows from the Sixties?"

"Yeah, sounds like her." Noticing the last rays of the sun disappearing in the west, I glanced at my watch. *Crap!* I was already forty-five minutes late for work. My boss must be having kittens by now. "Um, does she get hit often?"

The officer glanced up from his monitor and offered his warmest smile. "You'd be surprised."

"Surprised, I am already. How about filling me in? Is there a story here?" I wanted to talk, to hear him talk, to keep from thinking about my job or what just happened.

He pinched the bridge of his nose and sighed. "More like a legend." The officer looked to his left towards a thick grove of trees on the opposite side of the highway. "Just like a lot of stories out of that damn cemetery."

"Bachelors Grove, right?" Although I allotted ghost stories no more credence than I did the Easter Bunny, I shivered, and my heart felt as if it skipped a beat.

The officer's laptop cast a grayish-white light onto his face, making him look as if he himself was an earthbound spirit. He delivered his explanation in a way that made me think he'd related this tale many times before. "About fifty years ago, a girl named Daphne Wood from Oak Park died. Hit and run." His eyes met mine, like one Poker player looking for a tell in my expression. I hoped I didn't give him one that betrayed my skepticism. "Her best friend was Naomi Myers who lived all her life in Midlothian. Naomi was devastated when she got the news. She spent the next two days in hysterics before Mom and Dad called a doctor who gave her a sedative."

"Poor girl." I glanced at my watch again. The story intrigued me, but I wondered if I should interrupt my host to call my boss and tell him I'd be late. Really late … which he probably knew already. Instead, I decided to be a good guest and listen further. Besides, it sounded as if I wasn't a murderess after all, so now I could relax and just worry about my finances.

"Yeah." The officer tapped the laptop screen with his right index finger and studied something for a moment before resuming his tale. "Naomi woke up and realized it was past time for the funeral. She tossed on her favorite outfit without thinking, the one with the go-go boots, and ran to what she thought was Daphne's graveside service.

"Problem was the funeral was being held in Berwyn, as

in the opposite direction. Maybe she was too upset to think clearly, or the sedatives hadn't worked their way through her system. In either case, Naomi ran to the closest cemetery to her house."

"Bachelors Grove?" I felt my mouth go dry again.

The officer nodded slowly. "I guess she realized she was in the wrong place and ran out of the cemetery, probably hoping to get to the right graveside service in time. I suspect she wasn't checking for traffic – for all we know, she might have been blinded by her tears – but in any case, she ran right out into the street and a sedan hit her. Couldn't stop in time."

He pulled a half-full water bottle from below his seat and took a quick swig. "We get a report about once every couple of weeks about Naomi, still running out of the cemetery to find Daphne. Every time, the girl vanishes, just like with you." He gave the faintest of smiles as he replaced the plastic cap on his water bottle. "Don't worry. It's not like you killed her or anything."

"Can't kill the dead? That's a relief," I lied with a smile on my face. Between running down a dead woman and the threat of losing my crappy job, I had nothing about which to be relieved. But I hoped the policeman recognized my glibness wasn't a sign of anything more than the worst case of nerves ever. I rested my hands, palms-down, on top of my thighs. When I lifted them, two dark, wet handprints remained on my slacks. "So, what's next?"

"Okay, I have to file a report about this. Procedure, you know. You'll need the paperwork for the insurance company when you get that bumper fixed." The officer swiped a finger across the touchscreen of his laptop and studied a corner of the display with narrowed eyes.

He sighed and with an apologetic look, the officer said, "Now, about the matter of some unpaid parking tickets ..."

# # #

When I entered the telemarketing office, ninety minutes late, my supervisor awaited me in the doorway to the break room, preventing my access to the time clock. He ran a thick hand over his bare scalp in memory of a time when his hair grew wild and not just in his ears or along his upper lip in a thin salt-and-pepper line. A sneer pulled down the right side of his mouth as if it awaited one of those comically-huge stogies from some old cartoon. The expression in his eyes verged on being a hate crime.

After several grueling minutes of outlining my shortcomings in nearly microscopic detail, I was told that I would not be docked for showing up late. As a smile of relief grew on my lips, my supervisor informed me that I could just turn around and go home so I wouldn't be paid at all. I felt my joy evaporate and before I could describe my emotional ordeal with the vanishing corpse, he sadistically informed me that although the phone bank was a couple people short already, they'd muddle through the next three days without me.

"But sir," I growled, unwilling to give him the satisfaction of my tears, "I thought I killed someone on the way in. Well, turns out I didn't, but I still had to talk to the police who told me ... um, the officer told me I was in the clear, but I had so many unpaid parking tickets that he had no choice but to tow my car. Then before he could drive me here, just to be nice, he got a call, but had Dispatch send for a taxi instead. Then, because of the evening rush traffic, it took him half an hour to get to me ... and now here I am. Late."

My supervisor stared at me, visibly unmoved by my tale of woe. I said through gritted teeth, "I have a busted fender on a car I can't afford to pull from Impound. Now you're depriving me of three work shifts? Would ... you ... please ... reconsider?"

He crossed his arms. "If I reconsidered anything, it would be whether or not to let you work at all for the rest of the week. Now leave before I recall how little I like college punks who don't give a rip about their job, much less their employer's nerves. Good night." With that, my supervisor backed up just enough to slam the break room door in my face.

I practically ran outside to get away from the toxic atmosphere of this damned job.

No, the job wasn't damned … but I certainly was. I put in so much more time than effort to get my college diploma and look where I was today.

Nowhere. No money to afford a social life. No real friends. No direction. No future. And, no car.

I pulled my phone from my handbag and thumbed the device to life. I paused to look at the screen before hitting the power button again. And again. Then I held it down long enough to realize that the phone's battery was deader than the chances of a Republican becoming Mayor of Chicago anytime soon. So much for calling a taxi.

Dropping the phone into my purse, I walked towards the nearest street corner, attempting to recall the routes of the CTA buses this time of night. As I waited at the closest bus kiosk, all I needed now was a thunderstorm to make my night complete.

Enjoying the first break I'd gotten all day, the next bus took me to within two blocks of my apartment, the one I'd have trouble affording if I lost three days, or more, of work. Fortunately, it arrived on time and I actually had the correct fare. With minimal transfers, my travel home went as smoothly as anything had today.

Upon entering the apartment, I tossed my Goodwill jacket over the back of a Salvation Army chair. Once I kicked off my shoes, I strolled into the ludicrously tiny kitchen to my garage sale mini-fridge and the pitcher of grape-ade soft drink that awaited me. I didn't even have enough room in there, or the money, for beer.

My picture window afforded me a panoramic view of the apartment complex's parking lot. Leaning against my stove, embraced by the shadows of the room, I stared at the assigned space where my car habitually sat, sipping my generic grape drink from a cheap plastic tumbler as if it was champagne.

I wasn't certain if it was delayed stress from the accident or my temper elevating my blood pressure, but my head began to throb. I swallowed a couple of ibuprofen and pondered my finite financial options.

Now, I had three days to come up with a way to get my car back. I wouldn't even worry about what to tell the insurance company in the hopes my policy didn't cover damage created by ghosts. Assuming I could raise the deductible, of course. I momentarily relived the impact of Naomi's spectral body against my beloved vehicle. Then my headache intensified, my hands trembled, and I kinda wondered if this was what PTSD was like.

It wasn't like I could afford to ask a doctor right now anyway. I wasn't just broke, I was shattered. Sure, calling total strangers with the offer *du jour* didn't pay at all well, but at least it kept me in white-labeled, brown-striped sugar-free powdered fruit drink concentrate.

After the better part of an hour feeling sorry for myself, I decided that this whole escapade was Naomi Myers' fault. So tomorrow, I promised myself that I'd find her at Bachelors Grove Cemetery and give her a piece of my mind.

I found myself smiling as a plan formed in my mind. Perhaps I'd even find a way Naomi could make things up to me.

#

My body desperately wanted the release of dreamless sleep, but my mind refused to cooperate. After trying to get Mr. Sandman's attention for a few hours, I got up to visit the bathroom, then spent some quality time on my computer, researching this cemetery online.

At first, I shook my head at the numerous stories of ghostly women, vanishing houses, vampires, grave robberies, weird lights, possible Satanic rituals, ghostly vehicles of different eras, and an ax-swinging caretaker. Eventually, my smile vanished while the sun arose outside, and I realized just how many of these legends spawned from this single acre of land.

And yes, Naomi and Daphne's story could be found among those tales.

The sheer magnitude of tales from the last century and a half gave me pause. One or two hauntings, I could laugh off … but so many stories from so many people, not all of whom were crackpots, dabblers, and thrill-seekers. Some were reporters … genuine trained observers. I evolved from resolute skeptic to being open to having my mind changed and my terrors confirmed.

I also thought about my current situation of underemployment and a certain bleakness to my immediate future. As I educated myself in all things supernatural, post-dying existences, and this cemetery, a plan firmed up in my mind to pull in some quick money. Surely someone on YouTube would pay for an "expert" witness to a real ghost or two. Maybe I'd even tour those creepy horror conventions with a book I was sure I could get someone to publish.

As for Naomi and her search for her friend Daphne, they seemed to be common knowledge to the local police. That bore investigation, and I knew where to begin … and it wasn't at the Police Station.

#

Three cups of coffee, a change of clothing, and two CTA transfers later, I found myself watching the bus roar away to the north. A few minutes' more worth of walking and I'd return to the scene of my sort-of crime, a hit-and-run accident … except I wasn't the one running away from the area.

I approached the Bachelors Grove Forest Preserve with trepidation late the next morning. But then, I was just one more criminal returning to the scene of the crime. I hoped the fact of my checking on my victim would count in my favor somewhere down the road.

A couple of energy bars rested in my pocket and a

plastic water bottle swung from a belt loop in my jeans. As I approached the cemetery, I saw what I thought was a transformer or a switching station, erected by either the power or the phone company, I didn't know which. As I walked upon the uneven gravel in front of the cement block, I noticed a road that started a few dozen feet to the west. I approached the path with caution.

Steeling myself, I reached into my jacket pocket, reassuring myself that my surprise still rested inside. I whispered, "Time for a girl-to-girl talk, Naomi."

This path was too straight to be anything else but a road at one point in history, I guessed. As I walked over the bone-white gravel and infrequent strips of old asphalt, I studied the brown, twisted trees on either side of the path that formed a tunnel into which I strolled. "Naomi?" My voice cracked from the fear that incubated in my heart. "Daphne? Anyone?" But only the birds concealed in the skeletal, half-dead branches replied.

I said for years that I wasn't psychic, that I was totally insensitive to the paranormal. Today, however, I felt a presence surrounding me. The atmosphere felt thick and my breaths grew ragged while the air took on the musk of an old basement. Even the white noise of cars moving over the nearby highway refused to enter this dark place. Still, I forced one foot to move in front of the other.

Slices of gold cut through the wooden latticework above, offering a brief taste of warmth as I trod the pathway. I couldn't tell if my steps took me to the west directly or at an angle. All I knew was that every time I turned around, the limbs above and to either side of me appeared to weave even more tightly together, closing off my exit from this place.

Finally, I saw a clearing of sorts not too far ahead. The sun teased the edge of the gap in the trees on the west side of the property. I looked at my digital watch, but the face of my timepiece was blank. I shook my wrist and checked again before pressing the three buttons on the side of the device for all the good they did.

I bit my lower lip, something I seemed to be doing a lot since I got here. The watch could survive a trip to the bottom of a swimming pool, someplace I hadn't been recently. Also, I replaced the watch battery two weeks ago. With my current luck, I probably didn't keep the receipt for it.

I looked around, finding myself still alone, patted my jacket pocket, sighed with relief, then looked towards a small gap in the trees to the west of where I stood. However, my feet refused to move. I forced my legs to lift and when they finally obeyed me, I found myself taking a couple of steps towards my right … where I saw the cemetery for the first time.

The smell of freshly-cut grass clawed at my nostrils. The temperature dropped to where my ragged exhalations hung in the air, drifting slowly away like an indifferent ghost. I could easily walk towards the chain link fencing and the open gate that encircled the grounds. But when I tried to move towards the west again, my legs stiffened painfully. Finally, I surrendered to whatever forces ruled the property and entered the cemetery.

My heart hammered against my ribcage as I saw the infamous Pond at the far end of the property. Through the thick verdure past the pool of near-stagnant water, I could see, but not hear, glimpses of traffic on the nearby highway. Now inside the graveyard itself, I felt insulated from the mundane world, but not in a comforting way. Instead, my heart went cold as I realized how distant I was from any sort of help, should I need it. And a part of me knew beyond a certainty that I would.

The sparse number of headstones didn't surprise me after my online research. I stood in the center of the cemetery and listened. No birds ... no rustling of leaves ... no breeze whistling through the branches ... just the *boom-boom-buhboom* of my rapid heartbeat. I hesitated to break the unnatural silence, but slowly worked up the courage to whisper, "Daphne?"

No answer.

"Daphne?"

More silence.

A less inquisitive and far more grounded person might have left. No, they'd have sprinted down that aged roadway back to the real world with its exhaust fumes and racing engines and pollution and sweet, sweet ear-aching noise. They wouldn't be looking for a dead woman or her best friend.

Ah well ... in for a penny, in for a pound. Like the sweep hand of a watch, I slowly turned in place, my arms at my sides and my hands slightly elevated, palms up. I cleared my throat and spoke as confidently as I could, which was not a bar set high.

"Daphne. I call to you from the world of the living." I stifled a nervous giggle. I didn't know how some weekend amateur Ghostbuster might summon a spirit, but I received most of my paranormal cues from my older brother's comic book collection. I cleared my throat again, ready to skirt the edge of melodrama and re-establish the necessary dark mood. "Daphne Wood, I bring a message from your friend, Naomi Myers." I sighed, waiting for a reply that I expected would never arrive.

"What about Naomi?"

I gasped – no, let's be honest, I gave a little scream and I think I might have done something in my underwear that I hadn't done since I was an infant.

"What about Naomi?" The second inquiry sounded like her first, like an old 78 r.p.m. recording; a calm, youthful voice asking from behind a veil of scratchy vinyl, chilled midnight breezes, and half a century's worth of time.

Slowly, I turned to see a teenaged woman standing next to a weather-worn grave marker, her pale, placid eyes aimed just past my shoulder. Her hair was white and tied in a conservative bun at the base of her skull. She wore a threadbare dress edged with ivory lace that covered all but her dull, gray shoes, a dress that a mother might select for her daughter to be buried in.

But this ashen-skilled being was not the woman I collided with yesterday. I swallowed hard and forced myself to ask, "Are ... are you ... Daphne?"

She ignored my question. Her hand traveled to her brow and she gritted her teeth as if concentrating. "I heard you ... heard you talk about ... about Naomi. I ... I hear she ... she was looking for me ... I have ... have to find her ... make sure ... she is all right ..."

My heart raced. I fought against the urge to touch Daphne, to hug her, to reassure myself that she was real. "Naomi's looking for you. I don't think she can rest until she sees you. She's been asking for you ... um ... for a very, very long time."

At this point, I pulled my phone from my jacket pocket. I smiled to see that it still worked here, the digital readout on the face of the device ticking off the seconds that it recorded everything I saw and heard. I figured that one day, I'd question my sanity about Bachelors Grove, and I wanted evidence of this crazy, crazy day.

Besides, maybe I could write this up and make some much needed money in the process. It would be a fair reward for all I'd endured since the drive to work yesterday. It was my due, dammit.

Daphne looked around, her eyes wide with confusion, maybe fear? She didn't seem too concerned with her own state of existence so much as finding her friend. "Naomi? Are you here, sweetie?"

"I guess she's not here yet," I offered, holding the phone in my left hand to capture the ghostly cash cow before me. I glanced down to see Daphne's pale image in the view screen and forced down my own nervousness. "Maybe I could ask you a few questions?"

Ignoring me still, Daphne's gaze swung from one side of Bachelors Grove to the other and back. "Naomi? Please, Naomi. Let me know you're okay." She smiled as she called out in a voice unused for half a century. "I love you for looking for me. But I'm all right." Then Daphne suddenly turned her spectral attention to me. "She is okay, isn't she?"

Before I figured out how to tell her about Naomi's accident – well, both the one that did her in initially as well as my booster shot yesterday – the sound of a twig being snapped rang through the cemetery with the sharpness of a gunshot. Daphne and I spun towards the east at the same time.

A familiar long-haired girl stumbled down the shattered roadway once called the Midlothian Turnpike. Her knee-high go-go boot soles ground into the gravel as she cried out, "Where is Daphne? Where is Daphne?"

"Over here, Naomi! Over here!" I shouted.

The brightest smile I'd ever seen filled Daphne's face as she recognized her best friend. Then she turned towards me and appeared to be blinking back joyful tears, or what she remembered about the process of crying. "Oh, thank you, thank you, thank you. Pardon me, but I have to go now." With that, Daphne sprinted after Naomi.

A sudden fog filled my skull. I shook my head to clear it, but all I did was make it worse. But no matter. I knew I had to follow this adventure to its conclusion if I was going to find a way to exploit it fully, even if my concussion cried out for attention. I exited the cemetery, keeping the two girls in my phone camera's sight.

My left arm ached violently as I ran to catch Daphne and Naomi. I cried out for the women, but my irregular heartbeat was all I could hear in return. It even drowned out the sound of my own voice as I called out, "Daphne! Wait up, Naomi!"

Daphne caught up with Naomi at the far end of the path, almost within eyeshot of the highway. Daphne seized her friend's shoulder and spun her around.

Naomi turned to see her friend's grateful smile. She brought both of her hands up to her mouth in disbelief for her good fortune before throwing her arms wide and pulling Daphne into her embrace.

I ran forward, the phone in my trembling hand. I barely cared that the image probably looked as if I'd videoed it during an earthquake. I'd upload it when I got home, after I constructed a quick website and blog to document this encounter with the afterlife. Then after a while, I could monetize the site, maybe contact the local newspapers, perhaps hit the paranormal convention circuit, and tell my supervisor to go –

Daphne and Naomi held each other tightly, blissfully unaware of my approach. My footsteps hit the ground unsteadily, and I became aware of the painful drumbeat of my heart.

I ran towards the couple for a close-up, then stumbled through their gossamer bodies. I couldn't recall if my eyes were open by this point. All I knew was that I had to keep recording, even as I stumbled over the uneven ground, and towards the highway.

Then I heard a car horn sound just before something smashed into the left side of my body. I felt a sensation, not unlike flying, then rolling along the ground just before darkness overwhelmed me.

# # #

Not knowing how long I was out, I opened my eyes slowly.

I looked up into the face of a couple of EMTs, judging from their white jackets, each one adorned with a bright red corporate logo on the breast pocket. Behind the guys stood a middle-aged woman who stared down at me, wide-eyed and shaking with terror. The keys in her hand jingled as her hands trembled. No doubt they – both the keys and the lady – belonged to the sensible blue sedan behind her. I wanted to tell her my bumper had a crack in it too.

Turning my head slowly because doing so quickly sent excruciating pains shoot up and down the left side of my body, I glanced down towards my hips, but saw nothing but moist scarlet. In fact, I didn't see a whole lot of me there at all.

Looking up towards the woman again, I saw the policeman, the one who stopped me yesterday. I smiled to let him know I was okay – really, I was – that the pain in my head seemed to be subsiding. In fact, even though I felt a chill growing in my guts, my right hand could feel a pool of thick warmth under me.

I moved my lips to crack a joke and ease the tension,

but one of the EMTs cautioned me to remain silent. Could he do that? I thought that was the cop's job. Was I under arrest? Would the courts provide an attorney for me because I lost three days of work and couldn't afford representation? Funny how one's mind worked in times such as this, whatever those times were.

"You've been in an accident," the EMT stated patiently. "Please lie there. We are doing everything we can to stabilize you, so we can move you to a hospital."

But something in the man's eyes told me he was lying. I'm sure he wanted to get me some extra care, but something prevented it. I tried to move to a sitting position, but I couldn't. Neither EMT needed to place their hands on my shoulders, just like on TV, in order to render me immobile.

Then, I remembered Naomi and Daphne. I vaguely recalled them walking towards the entrance to Bachelors Grove Cemetery with the brightest smiles I could remember. Or did I imagine that? I had to know. Only one person could answer that for me.

I managed to whisper, "Whuh ... where is Daphne?" Then, my eyelids dropped, turning my world into midnight.

One of the EMTs said something about my blood pressure dropping while the other technician pressed a breathing mask onto my face. The woman emitted a shriek that should have shattered the ambulance's windshield. I opened my eyes in time to see her knees buckle and tears roll down her face. Fortunately, my friend the police officer caught her before she fell to the street. I'd even have loaned her an EMT if they didn't appear to be so intent on fussing over me.

Wanting to make sure this lady was all right, I asked the officer, "Where is Daphne?" However, he appeared to be distracted by the screaming woman. *Honey*, I wanted to tell her, *I know just how you feel. I felt the same way yesterday about this time*. But all that came out, again, was, "Where is Daphne?" which was also a valid question as far as I was concerned. In fact, I could think of no more important question at that moment, or the next.

One of the EMTs injected a huge needle into my chest that didn't hurt as much as I feared it might. In fact, I didn't feel chilly any more as much as I felt a gnawing curiosity about the fate of two certain girls.

I felt better than I had in years. I couldn't work up a scintilla of worry about my financial straits as I could conjure up the price of tea in China or Chicago or Narnia, for that matter. In fact, all I wanted was an answer to one question.

My phone rested on the street several feet away, the glass cracked, and the case dispersed in three unevenly-sized pieces. So much for making a profit on this adventure, not that it mattered to me any longer. I now had more pressing concerns.

Ignoring my earthly restraints, I rose to my feet.

Officer Friendly shook the hysterical woman while one EMT checked his wristwatch and mentioned something about the time of death. His partner turned off the oxygen tank that fed the poor woman lying on the pavement, her blood no longer oozing from her oddly-shaped midsection. She appeared familiar, as if I saw her face every morning in the mirror, but I had no time to identify the girl. I had new considerations and a question to ask.

I filled my lungs with air, or thought I did, and asked my question. But instead of offering an answer, the others simply turned towards where I now stood. The woman passed out in the officer's arms. Meanwhile, the wide-eyed EMTs scrambled away from me, pushing themselves backwards with their hands and feet, trying to put some distance between themselves and me.

In fact, everyone panicked but that twenty-something

woman lying on the asphalt, a huge hypodermic needle lodged in her chest.

The officer looked at me sympathetically. "Not you too."

I found myself racing into the woods, away from those fearfully pitying eyes, searching for the two women. I needed to ask them how their story ended. I knew Naomi would be too confused, the poor girl, so I felt compelled to ask someone with some real knowledge. I silently promised myself that I'd find those poor girls, no matter how long it took.

My old life faded from my memories as did my quest for easy money and my desires to comprehend the world around me. My mental and emotional needs simplified, coalescing into one specific craving.

I even forgot about the woman whose life I feared I'd stolen, just as another woman would now live with the regret of ending mine.

Now and forever, I ran up and down the dilapidated lane, my tears turning to mist, my old life forgotten. Time bleached my taut flesh and clothing. The only hunger I owned now was for an answer to the single question that consumed me.

The answer a small part of me knew I might never find.

"Where is Daphne? WHERE IS DAPHNE?"

SANCTIFIED

By

Brian K. Morris

In August of 1873, the natural decline in temperatures heralded the annual arrival of Fall. Farmers watched their fields, ready to harvest the crops in preparation for the inevitable survival of Winter.

Amidst the promise of September's arrival, a single brown horse pulled a simple buckboard wagon along a dirt road which bisected two rows of wooden homes in Midlothian, Illinois. With a tug on the reins, the driver stopped his horse to consult a map he'd purchased six states ago.

Beside the man sat a young woman, one that appeared to be at least twenty years his junior. Rachel Deeds held her open parasol upon her right shoulder, its matte black fabric serving as protection against the noonday sun. Her lean face tilted downwards, and her eyes stared at the floor of the wagon. Even her long, ebony hair fell in a straight line over her shoulders like foam over the rocks at the base of a waterfall.

As the driver spoke gently, occasionally studying his companion's outline with a slight smile, the girl remained mute except for when a wheel collided with one of the numerous ruts in the pathway. She closed her eyes and uttered a tight-lipped grunt as if she'd been personally struck. Overlooking her noises, the man looked from left to right and back again as he studied the village.

Stephen Wentworth emerged from one of the smallest clapboard houses in the township. With an agility that confirmed his entry into middle age was still many years away, he carefully navigated the ruts in the street until he reached the rig. "Good afternoon, sir. You appear lost," he stated cheerfully.

The wagon driver grinned. His full, white-streaked beard lifted alongside the corners of his mouth and his brown eyes twinkled. "I might not be, friend. Is this Bremen? Or are you still calling it Bachelders Grove?"

"Neither name any more." Wentworth pulled a square of gray cloth from a back pocket and wiped his hands with the fabric. After stuffing the handkerchief back in his pocket, Wentworth extended a hand. "Pastor Stephen Wentworth of Bachelors Grove, good sir. And your name is?"

The driver dropped from his wagon, sliding his hand into Wentworth's. "I'm The Right Reverend Josiah Clayton, late of the Kansas territory. Good to meet you, Mr. Wentworth."

"We're all on a first name basis here, Reverend." Wentworth shared a grin. "I'm the local pastor. I think it's because I read The Bible from cover-to-cover before anyone else locally. And your companion?" He turned his smile towards the girl.

"Her name is Rachel." Wentworth watched the young woman blush, smiling so briefly that he questioned whether he saw it occur at all. Clayton cleared his throat before continuing, "She's my niece. I never married, but my late sister asked that I adopt the girl upon her demise."

Rachel trembled briefly as she closed her eyes tightly.

Clayton patted Rachel's thigh. The girl shot him a quick glance before staring at the floorboard again. "Hello, sir," she murmured.

Wentworth smiled softly, nodding at the girl's guardian. "Always glad to meet another brother in God. There just can't be enough of us around here. I've been a widower for five years and it's good to see such a lovely face here." Wentworth drew his forearm across his forehead, then down each of his clean-shaven cheeks. "So, what brings you

185

through Bachelors Grove?"

"I understand you have a cemetery hereabouts, Stephen." Clayton waited for Wentworth to nod before he added solemnly, "The Lord God sent me here to sanctify the grounds ... before it's too late."

#

An hour later, Stephen Wentworth prepared dinner on a black cast iron stove, upon which a modest meat and vegetable stew gently bubbled softly inside a well-used pot. He'd turned down the bed in his bedroom and offered to sleep with a bedroll in his common room to maintain the young woman's propriety.

"Thank you, sir." Rachel gave another shy smile and a nod before dropping her chin once again.

The Right Reverend smiled. "Nonsense, my brother. If we must force you out of your own bed, I insist Rachel be in it."

Rachel's eyes flared, and her breath caught in her throat.

"And I," Clayton continued, not giving the girl a moment's notice, "will use my own bedroll. We've been doing this at every stop since we left Kansas. At least at the occasions where benevolent people like yourself would allow us to stay under a roof that didn't also accommodate barnyard animals." Clayton grinned in appreciation of his own joke.

As soon as everyone washed up, Clayton ladled a healthy portion of the stew onto the tin plates set before each person at the well-worn wooden dinner table. All three bowed their heads as Rev. Clayton spoke softly, "Thank you, Lord, for a safe journey, shelter, good food, and a new friend. May this food nourish our bodies, that we may worship you forever." Wentworth concluded his prayer with, "Amen."

More softly, a half second later, Clayton whispered, "Amen." Rachel licked her lips at the entrée's aroma and nodded gratefully when Wentworth passed a small loaf of bread to her, which she passed to Clayton after taking a small chunk for herself.

"Thank you, my dear." Clayton winked at Rachel who quickly turned her attention to the contents of her plate.

Eating quietly, save for the occasional scrape of steel fork against their plates, Wentworth completed his meal swiftly. Wiping his mouth before his company finished their bread, Clayton asked, "So what's this about the cemetery requiring sanctifying? I thought I'd done that with each funeral I presided over. Please don't tell me I've being doing this incorrectly."

Clayton chewed thoughtfully and swallowed before answering. "Most people, even those who've accepted the Lord, have difficulty hearing His still, small voice." Clayton's eyes locked with his host's. "I have heard that voice more than once. He led me to Kansas from Massachusetts, now to Illinois."

Wentworth chuckled. "Good thing I don't have an ego, Josiah. Otherwise, from not hearing the voice of God, I would think I'm not doing a good enough job." He grinned at Rachel, "I guess that's why it's called 'faith,' right?"

Rachel smiled quickly, then turned away shyly.

Laughing loudly, Clayton waved away Wentworth's self-depreciation. "I am certain that isn't true, my friend. But this is the calling I was given by our Lord and I go where He directs me."

Suddenly, Clayton's expression turned dark. "I have heard whispers of overwhelming evil seeking entry into our world from here, I don't know." He sighed. "God has a plan and I do what I'm told." Clayton blinked rapidly, a look of momentary confusion crossing his handsome features.

"As do we all, amen." Wentworth turned towards Rachel. "And what role do you play, dear Rachel?"

Rachel dabbed at her mouth with her napkin. But before she could speak, Clayton took his niece's hand in his.

"I fear that my niece is painfully shy. I apologize for any offense you may feel for she intends none."

"No offense taken, Josiah." Wentworth turned towards Rachel. "I will do my best to not embarrass you. I can't promise anything, though. It's been quite some time since I've had any company to speak of, especially the feminine variety."

In reply, Rachel's eyes glowed as they met Wentworth's. Her smile remained on her lips even after her face turned towards her lap once again.

Wentworth returned his attention to Clayton. "You both are welcome to stay as long as you like or need."

Clayton nodded with a smile just as Rachel's hand shot out like a snake, seizing her uncle's, and squeezing it painfully. Rachel fixed her gaze on a point in Infinity. "The cemetery calls us."

The Reverend cast a curious look at the girl as he tried to retrieve his hand. He muttered to the girl, "You haven't spoken this much since we left Kansas."

"Aren't you relieved?" Rachel whispered. With a confident look and sly smile, Rachel said slowly, "Perhaps I had nothing to say until this moment."

Clayton glanced at Wentworth, smiling weakly. "The girl has a gift from God. Her ear is tuned to the next world."

Rachel turned towards her uncle, squeezing his hand again. "Us. Now."

Clayton nodded, a frown growing on his lips and his eyes glazing over. He rose to his feet before telling his host, "We must heed the call. We shall return."

"Would you want some company?" Wentworth dropped his napkin beside his plate. "I can give you directions to the cemetery."

"We know where it is," Rachel stated firmly, her eyes narrowing as she looked at Clayton.

"We know where it is," Clayton confirmed. He slipped his hand from Rachel's grip with a neutral expression on his face. After seizing their coats and hats, the pair stepped through the front door and moved quickly to their buckboard.

Less than a half hour later, Clayton's wagon rolled up the dirt path to the cemetery's front gate. The sun slowly made its way across the sky, its dying light changing the underside of the clouds to scarlet. The horse looked one way, then the other as it neared the graveyard. As it turned back to look at Rachel, a low sound rumbled from its long throat as if trying to frame a warning.

"Easy, boy," Clayton said with an assurance he himself didn't truly feel. "We'll be resting soon."

The horse stopped twenty feet from the edge of the cemetery, refusing to move any closer despite his owner's urgings. With a resigned sigh, Clayton dropped from his seat onto the grass. He patted his horse's mane reassuringly. "We'll conduct our business quickly and get you back for a good brush down." He thought for a moment. "The Lord will provide and protect us all," he stated more for his own comfort than his animal's.

The horse snorted and brought its front hooves down hard onto the ground violently. Clayton studied the animal's antics for a few seconds. He reached for the horse, to pat its mane and offer comfort. But a glance at Rachel made the Reverend stay his hand.

Clayton moved to the other side of the wagon and helped Rachel descend to the ground. He took her hand as they entered the cemetery.

Rachel surveyed the grounds impassively. Her gaze danced over the handful of weather-marked wood and stone grave markers, then focused on the pond at the far side of the property. While her expression was calm, as usual, her eyes now held a newly-shown confidence that Clayton hadn't seen before. Rachel's gaze turned to meet Clayton's and she gave the brightest, widest smile she could.

Clayton grinned at the girl, then shook his head. A

sentence formed in his mind. *What happened back there? Why did I say what I did?*

But before he could utter a word, Rachel placed her index finger to her lips, hissing for him to remain silent.

Turning on his heel, Clayton cast his glance in all directions to make sure they were alone. He thought to himself, *Better put on a performance. Keep the grift alive. You never know who's watching.*

The Right Reverend Clayton dropped to one knee one step in front of Rachel before bowing his head. Clasping his hands together, Clayton stated with well-rehearsed reverence, "Heavenly Father, thank You for our safe journey to this place, this Bachelors Grove. Thank You for providing us with a friend and with shelter while we prepare to fulfill Your wishes." He inhaled sharply and surprised himself with the next words he spoke, "I await Your sign on how to proceed."

"You want a sign? I'll give you a damn sign."

Suddenly, talons dug into the sides of his throat. Clayton felt himself being lifted into the air until his legs dangled, leaving him unable to set his feet on the ground. The Reverend clawed at the slender hand, but could no more move it than he could a mountain.

"Stop struggling, you insect." From behind him, the

growl was feral, yet feminine. "Keep wiggling and I'll slit your throat. Now save your false prayers and attend me."

Clayton managed a brief intake of air as he struggled to catch a glance at his attacker. "Rachel?"

"Yes, your beloved … *niece.*" The girl's leer glistened in the dying light of the day's sun. "The one you attacked, the one you stole from her home, the one you threatened with violence if she revealed the truth to her own mother, the one you kept close to your side to prevent her from sharing her accusations with her mother and the law, and the one who supposedly heard the Voice … which is what I compelled you to say … and the one who guided you to this place, whispering your instructions as you slept, exhausted after repeating your crime again and again."

Rachel's tone turned serious. "Now be still and I'll set you down. But you will listen to me first."

Clayton went limp, tears streaming down his cheeks. A moment after complying, he felt the solid ground under his shoes again. He also felt the claws still dangerously close to seriously piercing his skin. "R-Rachel, what's wrong?"

"Not one thing. Not now," the Rachel-thing spat. "This little trollop lived a pious, boring existence. But one night – stop me if you've heard this one before – a false carrier of My Enemy's word found the widow Deeds oblivious to his awkward advances.

"Rebuffed, but still consumed with unrequited lust, a certain someone snuck into this little one's bed and hurt her … badly … someone she hoped would marry her lonely mother, and whom she trusted to keep her safe." Rachel grinned. "And you know who that was, don't you? Or were you too drunk to recall what you did … and how often?"

Sobbing, the Reverend managed to speak coherently. "You know I remember. Why do you torment me so?"

Rachel laughed. "Because it's *fun*, that's why!" Clayton could hear the sadistic grin mirrored in her voice. "Almost as much fun as those nights you slept under her mother's roof, your senses dulled by drink, but the fire of your passions stoked. You promised to marry this woman, to love her forever … but oh, how you looked at innocent Rachel. You knew she'd never want you, but you could never resist a challenge. Then one drunken night, she was innocent no more. You were so much stronger than this girl and –"

"QUIET!" The Reverend gathered his finite courage. "Who are you, demon? Can you not leave this girl be?"

"No more than you could." Rachel's voice grew serious. "Long ago, in lieu of honest work, you took on the guise of a deliverer of the hated Gospel. It was easy to prey on the helpless who called upon Him in their hours of greatest need, wasn't it? You are a confidence man, are you not?" After a few seconds of Clayton's frightened silence, Rachel leaned forward until her soul breath invaded the older man's nostrils. "*ANSWER ME!*" she growled.

"I a-am," Clayton managed to say. He took in a sharp breath. "My type's called a grifter."

Rachel smiled sweetly as her eyes narrowed. "Anyway, ten minutes after your vile deed against poor Rachel, you drank tea with her mother, hoping she wouldn't smell the alcohol on your breath. Somehow, you talked her into accepting your insincere apology for a moment of ill-temper with her.

"Meanwhile, the young girl you violated in her own bed prayed for succor from her shame and physical agony." Rachel's face twisted in mock sadness. "Poor girl. Not even a random angel gave the suffering waif a moment's notice." A slow grin crawled across the girl's lips. "Then in poor Rachel's desperation, she called out to anyone who could help her. *Anyone.*"

The leer returned as Rachel leaned close to Clayton's ear, her breath smelling of brimstone and decay. "So, I put myself inside her, right after you did. Since then, she's been a vessel for my powers and my purpose. Did you really believe coming here with the girl was *your* idea?"

Rachel's smile vanished once again. "I was selected because of my powers of persuasion. Otherwise, do you think any responsible mother would have allowed her only daughter to travel with an older, unmarried man, merely on a little girl's word? She heard my whispers too, you know."

Clayton gritted his teeth. "Wh-what do you want, demon?"

"I hear the dread in your tone, preacher." Rachel nodded with approval. "I like that." She wrapped her free arm around Clayton's chest, holding him in an embrace of iron. "In two days' time, because that will make three in this place and three is a number of great power, you shall pray over this ground, or so you will continue to promise aloud. Instead, you will recite the words I shall plant inside your unconscious mind."

As Rachel's words sank into Clayton's mind, she concluded, "Thus, *you* shall prepare this land for my brethren's arrival."

"*ME?* Why must you torment me so?" Clayton asked, his entire body shaking with terror.

Rachel spat a reddish-black wad of phlegm that landed with a wet thud at Clayton's feet. "Oh, the child rapist and chronic liar thinks I'm being mean to him." A chill wind blew across the back of Clayton's neck as Rachel growled,

"For what you've done in your life, Clayton, I'm better punishment than you deserve."

Feeling that false courage was better than no courage at all, Clayton asked, "What makes you think I will do as you wish?"

"One," the demon replied, "I don't 'think' anything. I am certain of the outcome." With that, she again lifted Clayton high into the air, cutting off his breath once more. Then she hurled the false reverend against a grave marker, shattering the wooden crucifix affixed to the top.

Painfully, Clayton turned around and found himself face-to-face with his captor.

"Look into my eyes," Rachel commanded as she closed the distance between herself and Clayton in small, quick steps.

Startled by the intensity of the demand, Clayton aimed his gaze at hers, hoping to challenge her control. In less time than he realized what a poor choice he'd made, the Reverend felt his will power, his very identity, vanish in the white-hot fury of the young woman's crimson eyes.

The demon in female form stated with full confidence, "For the next few minutes, you will hear no voice but mine until I release you." Clayton's knees buckled as she whispered, "You will not be able to speak of my plans to any soul, living or otherwise, until your tasks have been completed. Now, when I utter the following phrase ..."

Whatever Rachel said next drowned in the quicksand of Clayton's subconscious.

# # #

The steady rhythm of the wagon's swaying brought The Right Reverend Josiah Clayton to full consciousness. Bathed in the moonlight that turned the edges of the world to silver, Clayton inhaled a deep lungful of the night air and wondered if he'd been dreaming ...

... until Rachel squeezed his thigh. "Awaken, meat puppet."

Clayton turned towards Rachel, unable to meet her eyes. He could still feel her smile aimed at him, a smile that his kinder side feared would never appear again. With a quickly mumbled prayer, Clayton averted his gaze back to the road.

"Prayer?" Rachel asked sweetly. "And with a note of sincerity. That's a new one."

Such is my desperation, Clayton thought. Oddly, to him at least, his hands didn't shake with fear over his current state. In fact, he knew he projected no outward clue as to his dire predicament. Such was the power of the demon's enchantment.

Stopping in front of the Wentworth home, Rachel descended from the wagon to silently accept the reins from her guardian.

The horse's eyes went wide with what appeared to be fear. The animal refused to look at Rachel. Instead, it snorted and stamped at the ground once more as if Clayton could accurately decipher its actions.

But Clayton found himself calmly removing the bridle from the horse's mouth. He wanted to stroke his horse's muzzle, to comfort it with softly-spoken words. But he knew his actions were not his own.

Rachel glowered at the horse and whispered, "You know, beast. You *know* … for all the good it does you."

After Clayton unhitched the steed, Rachel led the horse behind the house to feed and brush the animal down. The horse turned towards Clayton, its dark eyes quietly pleading with its owner.

It wasn't the cemetery you feared, noble steed, Clayton thought. *It was her. Dumb animal, my backside. Certainly, smarter than me.*

Clayton allowed himself into the house, his mind racing in contrast to his measured physical movement. Once inside the house, he hung up his hat and jacket just as Stephen Wentworth entered the living room, carrying a candle to light his way. "Back so late? I was growing concerned."

I lied about Rachel being my niece. She's possessed by a demon who controls my actions and my voice. I can't warn you. I can't even show my terror. I need your help! Clayton wanted so desperately to say.

"I'm sorry to have worried you," Clayton stated instead. "Our trip to and from Bachelors Grove Cemetery proved longer than we'd hoped, not being familiar with the way and all." He automatically smiled as if all was well, which he knew good and well it wasn't.

Wentworth grinned sympathetically. "I get lost myself, every now and then and I've lived here for fifteen years." His smile vanished as his tone turned more thoughtful. "But lately, I feel uncomfortable around the cemetery, like something's up and about to happen."

"Don't be silly, Stephen." *It's nothing but evil, brother. Trust your instincts.* "Once I perform the consecration ceremony, everything will be fine." *I don't even know yet what I'll be doing, but I know it'll unleash some horror on this world. Help me.*

Clasping Clayton on the shoulder, Wentworth stated with determination, "Well, I'll be glad to watch an expert in action. Never too old to learn, right?"

"True." *Oh, you don't want to know what ... what I don't know, but scares me nonetheless ...* "This deed will be done in a couple of days, on this side of midnight. No sense both of us missing our sleep. I'd understand if you begged off." *Please help me! Pray for me! I can't tell you why, but I think God's the only one who can save me ... save everyone now. That is, if He truly exists ... and would hear the pleas of a scoundrel like myself.*

Both men were startled by the sound of a loud *WHHHEEEEEYYYYY!!!* followed by a loud *THUD!*

The two men exchanged startled looks, too bewildered to even move for a moment.

Seconds later, the back door opened, then closed again. Soft footsteps approached via the kitchen.

Rachel entered the candle's flickering sphere of illumination. Her eyes twinkled, and one corner of her mouth gently rose as she practically tasted the men's fear.

She spoke so softly that the men almost couldn't hear her. "Our horse. Heart gave out."

"I-I'm so sorry to hear that. I'll call someone to take care of the animal," Wentworth offered.

"That's fine," Rachel stated firmly. "Horsey isn't going anywhere. Not now." She forced her smile into submission as she looked into her faux uncle's narrowed eyes.

"P-perhaps in the morning?" Clayton wiped the sweat from his palms onto his shirt. "I think a good night's sleep will help us all."

Rachel smiled and nodded once before her expression turned neutral once again.

Wentworth placed his hand on Rachel's shoulder before dropping his head to pray.

"Dear Father," Wentworth suddenly jerked his hand from the woman. He blew on his reddened fingers, shaking them rapidly before he dared to check them in the candle's golden light. After a moment's examination, Wentworth sighed. "Weird. I felt as if my hand was on fire for a moment."

Rachel cast a dark glance at Clayton. "I'm going to bed." She spun on her heel and strode to the guest room confidently, as if ignoring the dark of the room.

Clayton wanted to warn his host, tell what little he knew in the hopes of Wentworth's counsel and assistance. However, due to Rachel's power, the Reverend followed the girl into the bedroom and closed the door behind him as if nothing could possibly be wrong.

Rachel sat up in a chair, watching Clayton intently.

"Why?" Clayton whispered.

"You liked him, right?" Rachel's eyes narrowed to

razor thinness. "You didn't even give the horse a name, 'Preacher.'" She stated the title as if a scorpion perched on her tongue. "Besides, it would be so easy to ride off to the west, just as you have so many other times." Rachel smiled, showing the barest hint of teeth. "Without horsey, you're stuck here."

Rachel leaned forward. She extended her hands so that the fingertips gently touched Clayton's temples and cheeks. He trembled, otherwise paralyzed by the woman's eyes.

"I'd better ensure that flight will be the last thing your body can do." Rachel's thin nose almost touched Clayton's. "Hear my words … feel my power over your body … but first, get comfortable." She smiled again. "I'm in the mood to play, puppet."

Swallowing hard, Clayton removed his shoes before lowering himself to the floor, fearing the nightmares to come.

# # #

The next morning, as pink and crimson streams of eastern light announced the new dawn, The Right Reverend Clayton woke up sweating inside his bedroll. He opened his eyes to see Rachel still staring down at him from her chairside vantage point. He pulled the blanket up to his face to wipe his brow.

Although she appeared as fresh as if she'd gotten a good night's sleep, Clayton couldn't be sure if she'd slumbered for even a moment. *Do demons even require sleep?*

Her emotionless eyes followed Clayton as he splashed water on his face. Sighing as his knees creaked, the man gathered his clothing for the day with shaking hands. He couldn't recall all that occurred the night before, and wasn't certain how much he genuinely wished to remember.

Clayton dressed in silence and soon emerged from the guest room to see a note. "Don't bother reading it," a voice commanded.

The Reverend turned to see Stephen Wentworth emerging from the kitchen. "I just got back from making arrangements to have your horse taken away. I'm so sorry about the poor beast. Anyway, I left that note to tell you I was going to be out."

"Thank you," Clayton said, his tongue as numb as his heart. "Fortunately, we have some savings and can buy another today if you can guide me towards a reputable stable." The corners of his mouth turned upwards as he said, "Besides, it's not like we are leaving right this minute, unless you're tired of our company."

"Don't run off on my account." Wentworth glanced at

Rachel who entered the room a moment earlier, her head bowed, but her eyes watched the men. "It's been nice to have company. I haven't had much of that since my wife died. Didn't make it through childbirth, the poor woman."

Clayton bowed his head, but not before catching the sly smile on Rachel's lips. He shivered inside at the cruelty in her expression. "If you don't mind, we'll be here at least a couple more days."

"That agrees with me," Wentworth said happily. His smile faded as he glanced towards the side of his guest's neck. "Did you cut yourself shaving?"

Clayton said quickly, "Mosquitoes must love the flavor of Kansas blood."

Wentworth nodded slowly as he noted the size and even spacing of the reddish-cuts. "Let's have breakfast, all right? And if you're of a mind, I have some rounds to make among my flock. You both are welcome to accompany me, and we'll get you a new steed before noon." He grinned, with a glance towards Rachel. "Although I'm not a big advocate of temptation, you understand, I'd love to entice you to sticking around for a while."

"Sounds great." *No! Hell is coming tomorrow night and you're going to make me meet the victims of the perfidy I'm about to commit. Why can't I give a clue as to my distress?* Clayton smiled softly as he excused himself to get his coat, hat, and Bible.

Minutes later, the three of them walked at the edge of the street with Rachel two steps behind, staring at the back of Clayton's neck. The two men engaged in small talk until they reached a dry goods store. The name "CLANCY'S" spread across a plank suspended above the three pine steps that led into the store.

At that moment, a pair of elderly ladies emerged from the building, each carrying a basket topped with a small white doily concealing the contents. They whispered to each other, almost simultaneously until one of them caught a glance of Wentworth. When she stopped, so did her companion.

Wentworth turned to his guests and their inquisitive expressions. "The Gale Sisters, Elaine and Eloise. Never married, knows everyone's business, deaf as doornails." He turned to the sisters, speaking with enough volume to be heard inside the store. "Good morning, ladies. I trust you are both well."

"Yes, we are, thank you." Eloise, the elder of the two, exposed her brightest smile at the preacher. Her younger-by-two-years sister followed suit. Almost immediately, their attention swerved towards the Right Reverend, which made the man oddly uncomfortable.

A minute later, introductions were exchanged with smiles and handshakes all around except for Rachel who nodded and never took her dark, unblinking eyes from the sisters, nor did she extend her own slender hand in new friendship.

"Consecrating the cemetery?" Elaine's smile shone like sunlight on a lake. "That sounds exciting, in a sacred sort of way."

It's not sacred, Clayton thought. *I am sure I will be defiling the land and creating a horror I dare not imagine. I am frightened and alone and can't say a word to you. RUN! RUN FOR YOUR LIVES!*

But what Clayton uttered with a sincere smile was, "You know, it might be interesting, after all." He turned to Wentworth and then to Rachel whose lips moved almost imperceptibly. However, the Right Reverend heard her words in his head a split second after the girl uttered them under her breath, and he repeated them in turn.

"The ceremony will be at midnight, tomorrow. The Lord is glad to show off His great works to reaffirm His power and His majesty. And to those who do not believe, let them gaze upon His work and cast their sins aside to be washed in the blood of the Lamb."

Even Wentworth's jaw dropped at the intensity of Clayton's words. "Amen, my brother," was all he could whisper in response. "What made you change your mind about having an audience?"

Clayton shrugged as he watched Rachel wrestle her smile into submission.

# # #

"Consulting your Bible, oh ministry fraud? What a noteworthy occasion."

Inside the room they shared, Rachel watched Clayton study The Good Word more intently than he had done in years as research for his grift. He sat, cross-legged, on the floor, hunched over his Bible as if ready to physically dive into its pages for sanctuary.

Clayton's "niece" smirked at him from the center of the bed, pulling her legs up under her. "Did you check that book on the night you took this meatbag's innocence? Did you pray for forgiveness?"

"The latter, I have done every day since I committed the foul deed," Clayton admitted, his teeth grinding. *Although I allowed myself to be distracted by your – the girl's beauty as well as my baser desires. What in the hell was I thinking?* "Allowing me to speak freely, are you?"

Rachel nodded. "It amuses me. I control your actions,

208

but cannot consistently read your thoughts. I must say, though, your terror is delicious. I could lick the sweat from the back of your neck like a fine wine." She grinned. "You just might enjoy me doing so, I bet. Evidently, you had more plans for this body." Rachel frowned. "Although you haven't touched it for days ... and I've given you every opportunity."

Clayton felt the shame of his deeds burning his heart as it was dipped into molten iron. "I didn't want Rachel to tell her mother." He blinked away his tears. "I hate myself."

"As well you should. However, while you didn't have to take a bite of the apple, so to speak, I think you underestimate my persuasive ways. I'll take as much credit for your current situation as you take the blame, puppet." Rachel sounded almost hurt. "Now, tell me what's on your finite mind." A stern look crowded any aspect of pleasantness from Rachel's face. "Tell me now."

"Tomorrow night," Clayton confessed. "I am nervous about my role in the proceedings." He turned his eyes to his Bible again, now regarding it as more than just a prop.

Grinning, Rachel stated, "It has all been pre-arranged, and the words planted deep in your mind. Your sheltered existence probably never prepared you for terms like 'ley lines' or 'convergence points' or even 'hellmouths," did it?"

"Can't say it did, demon." Clayton closed his eyes and

mouthed a silent prayer for forgiveness. He visualized a supreme being filled with unimaginable power and limitless forgiveness listening to his pleas, one that Clayton hoped didn't turn His mighty back to this worthless sinner.

"Stop it!" Rachel hissed, pressing her hands over her ears. "The words burn!"

Clayton smiled. "So, you can't control me completely, eh?"

Rachel's lips pulled back as a feral *hsssss* escaped her mouth. "My activities have rules set down by my Adversary and Creator. As He allows it, I must grant you a certain amount of free will." Her eyes met Clayton's. "No matter what you do or say. Your actions are set in stone."

"All of them? All my future misdeeds?" Clayton found enough courage to fix his grimmest stare at the demon child.

The girl pulled herself into a ball, staring at her thrall from over her knees. "All right, there are rules that could save you. Nothing says I have to tell you what they are, though." Rachel's eyes dipped into shadow, then reappeared. "Instead of threatening me, are you up for a deal, human?"

"I would never enter a deal with you, temptress." A deep breath later, he whispered, "But, simply out of curiosity, what do you offer?"

"Immortality." Rachel smiled. "I see by your eyes that

you are intrigued."

Hoping his poker face would suffice, Clayton stated, "I'm listening."

"Just allow my master this one acre of Bachelors Grove and you will survive. You have my word." She uncurled and considered the preacher like a cobra sizing up its prey. "Your life for some strangers. They die swiftly, you live forever." She raised a finger for emphasis. "And I won't bother you a day further. What say you?"

Clayton pursed his lips in concentration. After a couple of minutes, he said hesitatingly, "I would need time to contemplate this."

Rachel nodded. "I fully understand." She smiled softly. "In fact, as the ceremony unfolds, you will have an opportunity to either seal the deal or reject it completely." The woman's face seemed to draw shadows from the very air itself. "But you will know when the point of no return occurs, when you will have no choice. No choice at all."

An oppressive silence filled the air as Clayton weighed his options and the potential consequences of his compliance.

"Would you please leave?" Rachel smiled as she pointed towards the bedroom door. "The stench of your indecision makes me gag." The smile vanished. "Now, go!"

Clayton pulled himself to a standing position and left the room without a backwards glance, not certain if doing so was of his own volition. He closed the door silently behind him.

Walking into the common room, Clayton noticed deep yellow beams of sunlight coming into the windows. *Not long before this community is eternally damned.* However, he allowed himself a spark of hope. *But her power over me isn't absolute. I have a chance of emerging whole from this, maybe even profitable.*

Suddenly, shame and sorrow overwhelmed the faux preacher. *The demon was right. The life span of this community can be measured in mere hours and here I worry only about my own safety and prosperity. How base a creature am I?*

Before an answer could present itself, the front door of the house opened, and Stephen Wentworth entered. He slipped out of his jacket and hat to deposit them on a pair of pegs set into the wall.

Catching a glance at his houseguest, Wentworth smiled. "Not getting a case of nerves, are you? It's a large task our Lord has set before you."

"It's nothing I asked for," Clayton stated with total conviction. "But, I truly have no choice in the matter."

Wentworth clasped his guest's shoulder. "None of us do when we serve The Lord. You are truly blessed with a higher destiny, my friend." He sighed. "I wish my own faith was stronger. Perhaps I would be – no, that's the sin of Pride talking. I apologize."

"No apology needed, sir. Your faith towers high above mine."

Wentworth averted his gaze, almost shyly. "Would you do me an honor, my brother?" He smiled. "May I pray with you?"

Shocked into speechlessness, Clayton could only nod. Smiling happily, Wentworth bent his knee and guided his new friend to a kneeling position. Clayton watched, hoping to learn how a genuinely pious man sought divine council.

Wentworth's head bowed, and he closed his eyes. "Heavenly Father, in your infinite wisdom and compassion, please bless Brother Clayton and his niece in this sacred task. I pray You give this man the strength he requires as well as the protection against the forces of evil that would stand in his way." He concluded with a gentle, "Amen."

The preacher looked up to see tears rolling down Clayton's face. Rubbing his sleeve over his eyes, Clayton whispered, "I've never been prayed for, Brother Wentworth. It was beautiful. Thank you so much."

"Really? I can't imagine a good man alive who never knew the comfort of another person's prayer."

Clayton excused himself and exited the house rapidly, much to his host's astonishment.

Soon, Clayton found himself wandering down the streets of the community, his head swimming at the enormity of the task before him and the consideration of his limited defenses. He wiped the sweat from his face, almost hoping Rachel's influence prevented his overwhelming guilt from showing.

Having followed Wentworth on his rounds, many of the locals recognized Clayton. The Right Reverend in assumed name only returned the smiles beamed towards him. He nodded in greetings, even stopping to shake hands and to humbly accept their gratitude for his presence.

Instead of invigorating him, each kind word tore through Clayton like a knife's edge, slicing into his very soul.

How can that amazing man have so much faith in something he can't see or touch? I suppose if I had some kind of firm evidence of a God, I might want a taste of that pure joy he obviously feels.

Clayton smiled gently and tipped his hat as he passed a young couple emerging from a dress shop. The young lady, who couldn't have been too much older than Rachel, absolutely glowed as she looked into her companion's eyes with an obvious devotion that other men could only envy.

Dabbing at his eyes with the back of his sleeve, Clayton thought, *Why do I see nothing but joy when I feel such misery? Why do I feel like a total worm in Wentworth's presence? He's warm, respected, contented with his life ... everything a miserable liar and user like myself could never be.*

Finally wandering to the far end of the village, beyond the last houses of the community, The Right Reverend Josiah Clayton stopped and listened for the sounds of humanity ... laughter, horses pulling their carriages, singing, anything. However, none of those noises reached Clayton's ears, which was just fine with him.

Satisfied that he was alone, Clayton dropped to his knees and clasped his hands together. He lifted his face to the clouds and spoke with more sincerity than he believed possible. "Please ... I know I've taken Your name in vain ... passed myself off as Your servant ... but I need Your help, assistance I don't deserve ... I'm weak ... I don't want to die ... I don't want to destroy this community ... I don't know what to do ... I know I'm not worthy of Your attention, but I need a sign, just one crumb of Your grace. Please ...

215

PLEASE answer my prayer." Clayton wept unashamedly as he listened intently, hoping desperately for a sign he knew he didn't deserve.

The birds sang. The breeze pushed its way through the leaves in the trees. But no wisdom filled Clayton's mind. Nor did he expect it to.

However, regardless of its origin, a determination now burned in Clayton's mind to challenge his captor, no matter the consequences.

Clayton usually took a nap in the late afternoon when he knew he might have to keep later hours than normal. This usually meant tent revivals, and the midnight hours needed to flee the county once the services ended. Sometimes, it meant "comforting" his troubled female parishioners as long as his strength, to say nothing of their savings, endured.

Knowing the gravity of the approaching midnight service in the cemetery, Clayton planned to be tired, possibly slow in his reactions. *Any disadvantage I give myself can only help.*

Clayton contemplated his days of masquerading as a man of the cloth as he sat at the kitchen table. As a teen, he read his first dime novel to get a taste of life beyond Missouri. After that, Josiah Clayton never again entertained the notion of working the family farm. It would be the grifter's life of travel and adventure for him, just like he read about in the books his friends loaned him.

He wasn't exactly hard on the eyes to most females, but not so handsome as to make their menfolk suspicious and jealous. Plus, he quickly learned how to read the tells, the unconsciously provided clues to a person's innermost thoughts and inevitable reactions. This served him well at the local saloon and their corner table Poker games, but now Clayton set his sights on bigger antes.

Then one day, after reaching adulthood, Clayton recalled a travelling preacher who erected a tent on the edge of town many years before. The reverend held a fire-and-brimstone faith meeting that proved entertaining for the lad. To his mom, the stranger offered a path to Salvation and convinced her to empty her pocketbook into the collection plate for a place on that road. Being a youth filled with wanderlust, desire for easy money, and a vivid imagination, Clayton felt he could do that too.

Starting small, Clayton stole a horse and wagon from the farm and travelled west. After getting a little seed money from some of the Faithful, Clayton invested in a collar, one that a prostitute in Springfield, Illinois sewed for him during her off-hours. Now disguised, Clayton's grift became smoother and smoother over the next fifteen years.

Then one night, after too many "little nips" from a bottle of white wine, Clayton felt the urge to fill a young parishioner with more than the Holy Spirit. Fueled by his success, Clayton attempted to repeat the process during his journeys just as fervently as he worked to fill his wallet.

Unfortunately, that proved to be how he damned poor, sweet Rachel as well as himself.

Just as that dark thought crossed his mind, Clayton looked up to see Stephen Wentworth enter the room. The man wore his whitest, least worn shirt and a freshly-laundered vest. "Good evening, brother."

Clayton found himself grinning. "You look like you're going out on a date. Anyone I know?"

"Sorry, but I'm excited." Wentworth checked the buttons on his shirt cuffs. "I don't mind telling you that all of Bachelors Grove is abuzz about this. I don't know too many people who won't be attending. In fact, the Gale Sisters plan to be up way past their bedtime to see this. It's like the whole town's under a compulsion to be at Bachelors Grove tonight."

Clayton felt his jaw muscles tighten. However, Rachel's spell forced his head to bob up and down. "That's good to hear," he said with unwilling conviction. "I promise this night will change everyone's lives forever." *That's what I'm afraid of.*

Wentworth's smile softened. "I wish I had your kind of faith, Josiah." He waved his hands excitedly. "No, no, not for my ego's sake. I mean I wish I was the kind of man that changed lives. I'm sure you never get tired of being a good influence."

Swallowing hard, Clayton managed to smile. A tidal wave of shame fell over the Right Reverend. He couldn't recall ever having one true friend in this world. If he wasn't under a compulsion to act out this role as Rachel's lackey, he would surely weep. Again.

At that moment, the bedroom door swung inward. Rachel exited the room, her eyes alight with anticipation. "It's time to go."

With those words, Clayton felt "Rachel's" dark powers overwhelm his senses, drowning all conscious control. The fake pastor almost leaped to his feet to seize his coat and hat. Wentworth's gait was far less speedy. Soon, the three left the house for an appointment with destiny.

Clayton surveyed the crowd outside Wentworth's home and his jaw dropped with astonishment. Wagons lined the length of the street and pedestrians filled the gaps between them. Light from a hundred or more lanterns and torches cast a golden glow that warmed the night. Horses snorted and scraped their hooves over the ground as if urging their owners to make haste.

Rachel bared her teeth at the horses, her fists clenched.

Sweat pouring downward into the back of his collar, The Right Reverend Josiah Clayton helped Rachel into the buckboard before climbing up himself. He seized the reins in his sweat-coated hands and turned to his audience, wishing desperately to be able to tell them to run, to save themselves.

Instead, the entranced Clayton smiled as he turned to address the populace. "Follow me!" he cried and with a tug on the reins, his new horse moved forward towards Bachelors Grove Cemetery, leading the population of the community to their inevitable damnation.

Josiah Clayton guided the wagon towards the road leading to the cemetery. Like the horse whose reins he held tightly, the man felt constrained by Rachel's Satanic compulsion. Behind him, people sang hymns of salvation and celebration, causing Rachel to tremble as if in the grips of a palsy.

"Make them shut up," she growled so softly that only Clayton could hear her. "Their praise to my Enemy burns my ears like molten brass."

"We're almost there," the Reverend stated while suppressing a small smile. *I feel no compulsion to silence the crowd's hymns. Good to know you feel real pain, monster. I can use that.*

A grifter makes his living by knowing his clients' boundaries, and then either finding a way around them or busting right through them. Time to work the biggest grift of all! "I'm sure their mournful cries will end soon," Clayton stated without looking at his companion.

Several hymns later, The Right Reverend and Rachel pulled up to the front gates of the cemetery, their entourage halting as well. Clayton turned around to see Stephen Wentworth atop his horse, the man's eyes wide with expectation.

Clayton stood up to address the crowd, his arms raised towards Heaven as if pulled by unseen strings. He cleared his throat as the walking locals stopped shuffling and those who rode coaxed their horses to silence.

"My friends," Clayton shouted, his hat casting a shadow over his features, "we have assembled to witness a momentous occasion. The Moon above illuminates an event that shall change your lives ... all of our lives."

Clayton dropped his gaze towards Rachel who grinned with ecstatic anticipation. She tapped her feet impatiently as her eyes played over the cemetery grounds.

"But I must ask you," Clayton continued, "to remain outside the gates until my niece and I complete our task." He smiled. "Believe me, you'll know when we are done."

With that, Clayton lowered himself over the side of the buckboard. Rachel didn't wait for any sort of assistance. By the time Clayton's boots touched the grass, Rachel stood in front of the horse, motioning for her "uncle" to join her.

In response, Clayton walked unhesitatingly to her side. Rachel's commands took full hold of his mind, leaving him a mute observer of his own actions, unable to interfere or influence the inevitable outcome.

Clayton linked his fingers with hers and they strolled together through the gates and into the cemetery itself. He looked neither left nor right as he walked to the center of the grounds.

Stepping over the uneven earth, Rachel murmured, "Be patient, 'Uncle' dearest. Soon, your role shall be fulfilled, and your will restored." She chuckled. "All the better to savor your genuine reactions to the events to come. And then I'll have your decision."

Standing in the center of the grave markers, Clayton and Rachel turned to face the iron gate and the anxious populace beyond. Stephen Wentworth stood at the forefront, a sentry denying his village entry to the burial grounds. His eyes reflected a large amount of curiosity and wonder with just a hint of envy.

Rachel turned her eyes towards the sky and the full Moon above. She drunk in the power from those soft, ivory rays for a moment. Without looking at her helpless meat puppet, Rachel whispered softly, "Now."

Unable to control his actions, Josiah Clayton lifted his hands towards the skies. However, instead of the open palms of supplication, his fingers twisted into a gesture that pre-dated all human life, lost to time until now. He filled his lungs and cried out, "To those hosts who would enter this sacred space, we call out."

"Enter, curious spirits," Rachel sang boldly, her eyes glowing with almost lewd delight.

"Sink your talons deep into this land." Clayton felt an icy breeze slap his face. "Gather the invisible forces that convene on this acre of soil. Infest this soil with your delicious pestilence. Drive out the light to pour your brimstone and deviance into the land itself!" Then several words escaped the grifter's lips, words in a language he couldn't identify.

"Excuse me?" Wentworth's voice cut through the rising volume of the chilly winds that tugged at every woman's skirt with frightening velocity. The men behind the preacher clutched the brims of their hats in an attempt to maintain ownership. But Wentworth's concern was less with his headgear than with the bizarre turn of weather and the words that rang oddly in his ear. "Brother Clayton?"

Rachel's hips swayed suggestively as she stared up at Clayton. She licked her lips, almost as if savoring the evil in the air. "Continue."

"Connect this world to the next," Clayton commanded the unseen forces around him, a seed of evil planted inside him now growing and bursting through his soul. "Build a tunnel of magic and corruption that it may flood this world with your offal."

Rachel's voice floated upon the chilled winds, "The man who beseeches you is a rapist, a molester, and one a liar who takes advantage of the weakest of mortals to meet his own selfish needs. He is truly the vilest of beings, now pressed into your unholy service. Lend him your loathsome might to consecrate this soil for the darkness."

Thunder sounded in a cloudless sky, driving the villagers to huddle together in confusion. Clayton felt all that was good in his heart vanish, smothered by memories of the vile past that led him to this moment.

The soil beneath Clayton's feet rolled and the pond

behind him gurgled like a woman choking. Mocking laughter from a thousand condemned souls danced on the howling winds. A pause in Clayton's recitations gave the man a moment to think freely:

Damn your endorsement, demon. I've never lost a grift to anyone since I fled that farm. A seed of courage cracked open, nurtured by pride and a surprising desire to see justice done. *I won't lose now! I swear to God, I won't give up. If You're up there, God, I need some help down here.*

Clayton listened to his surprisingly even heartbeat. *Wait for your moment. Find that instant of hesitation, of doubt ... she will have one ... everyone does ... then work it like the grifter you are.*

Dozens of yellowed, skeletal hands pushed through the cemetery soil, groping for a handhold on the grass.

At one corner of the grounds, barely a dozen feet from the pond, a stone edifice emerged from the very soil itself like a stalk of corn hewn from marble. Clayton recognized the building as a crypt although the markings on its exterior were not in any language he recognized.

From inside the tomb, the sound of talons scraping against stone and inhuman laughter filled the air.

Beyond the fencing, Wentworth pulled away from the hands that clutched his clothing, innocent witnesses to this travesty, all hoping the preacher's own faith could shield them also. However, as he approached the iron gates, a cloaked being pushed free of the soil and slammed the iron door in the preacher's face, smashing his nose, and knocking Wentworth backwards into the arms of his parishioners.

The being's hands shared only the barest similarities to those of a human being's. Seizing the gate again, whatever passed for flesh burned as it contacted the iron. Despite the increasing force of the wind tearing through Bachelors Grove, the dirt-colored hood remained in place over the being's features.

Pulling the gate open once more, the thing leaped forward and confronted a couple who owned a farm at the edge of town. The man and wife stared in horror as the *thing* pulled back its hood, exposing its true features to them.

In unison, the husband and wife emitted a scream that ended only when their hearts exploded in their chests from the sight before them. They dropped to the ground, lifeless and free of the horrible visage of the demon.

The *THUD* made by the bodies barely decayed when the demon stepped over the female and lifted her by the hair. With a mighty yank, the creature dug its talons into her skull and tore the woman's body in two from scalp to waist.

Clayton witnessed a wraith exiting the form which

floated above the body, bound to the cooling flesh by a silver cord fastened to the specter's navel. If one looked at the apparition closely, after wrestling down their fear sufficiently, one might see the spirit's features twisted in horror, her eyes unable to look away.

Ignoring earthly physics, the demon stepped into the woman's body, sliding it on like a snug pair of trousers. Once the flesh was pulled tightly together, a golden fire spread along the length of the wound, knitting the sundered skin until not even a scar remained. The apparition faded as a grimace crossed the earthly counterpart's lips that now pulled back to expose a pair of razor-sharp fangs.

"Yessss," hissed Rachel, who danced to the music of demonic screaming. "Drink deep, my fellow demons. Nourish yourself on the warm, rich wine of human life. Embrace your new vampiric forms."

Just then, the crypt door swung outward, and a score of hooded demons emerged. Smelling the heady, sour aroma of fear and blood, they scampered like rats across the cemetery grounds towards the terrified villagers, some of whom had just now recovered their wits enough to flee … but not enough of them.

Those villagers who remained were swiftly surrounded by the monsters who swiped at the humans with their scalpel-like nails, opening warm flesh, exposing bone, and drawing blood with every slash. Some of the hooded creatures ignored the easy prey to gallop down the road, losing themselves in the night.

Slowly, Clayton felt his full reason returning. He trembled with fear as he witnessed the carnage. Turning towards Rachel, his terror gave way to a mounting sense of rage. *Dammit*, he thought, *I control the grift. NO ONE USES ME!*

His open hands knotted into fists as he approached the girl.

Hugging herself, Rachel laughed at the frightening scenario playing out in front of her. "Didn't I tell you I'd find a way, my brethren? Didn't I promise to bring you into this world of frightened meat and thick blood? Did I not swear to bring you a feast of despair? Enjoy, my fiendish allies. Savor our triumph."

Then she caught a glance of Clayton as he approached her. She smiled, almost lovingly, at her former toy. "Ah, you've fulfilled your purpose. I must thank you for your cooperation, Clayton. Watch my fellows as they ... how would you say it? ... work the crowd." She cast an admiring glance at the hooded demons who circled the remaining villagers. "The merging to form the vampiric hybrid often goes more smoothly when the subject is cooperative, even volunteering. I can hear some of the townspeople begging for their lives, offering what they feel is valuable in exchange. Heh, what some people will do for power."

Clayton found himself staring at the scene beyond the fence. Several villagers broke away from the crowd, pleading for mercy and vowing compliance in exchange for being allowed to live and to serve. For their pleas, many were physically ripped in twain to become the new flesh suits for their demonic controllers. The rest struggled in the embrace of their vile captors who held them fast.

What do any of us have to offer immortal beings?

Soon, even more demons emerged from the stone crypt like pus from an infected wound. They might rapidly outnumber the inhabitants of the village, Clayton guessed, ready to spread their corruption beyond the village limits.

"In case you're wondering," Rachel offered, bowing at the waist with a flourish of her hands, "you're still under my protection. Since you were *soooo* helpful, I'd like to now offer you that gift I mentioned earlier."

Clayton pulled his eyes from the carnage beyond the gates. "How generous of you." He stifled a gasp as he saw the girl's transformation. Rachel's eyes swam in shadows and her lips took on a scarlet fullness that begged to be smothered in lustful kisses. Her fingers lengthened, and her nails turned into crimson blades

Rachel shrugged off the sarcastic compliment. "I know you plot against me. I can see it in your eyes. After all, you're *only* mortal." The woman now spoke in more human tones, warm in their inflection for the first time since the night he took her innocence. "Please hear me out, Mr. Clayton. I offer you an existence free of fear and pain." She took a step closer to Clayton. "All you need to do is enter my embrace. What do you say?"

Clayton looked at the crypt, then the mob of monsters parading outside the gate. Unable to witness the carnage any longer, he turned towards Rachel, whose curves seemed to mold themselves into a womanlier shape as Clayton watched.

He inhaled deeply and let out his breath slowly. "A hug for life eternal, huh? That's quite a deal." Clayton contemplated the offer for another few seconds, then laughed heartily. "My dear, I'm a grifter. I know a shady offer when I hear one because I've initiated many a similar deal against the unwary. I'm afraid I need more assurances as to your sincerity. After all, I hear your boss is the original king of the grift himself."

Rachel threw her head back and cackled. "You are

privileged to have even one choice. You either agree to accept my proposal, or you share the fate of your fellow humans." She pointed to the gateway of the cemetery. "That's one more option than they received."

Casting a quick glance at the remaining citizens of the township, Clayton saw Elaine Gale stretch her now-powerful arms towards the skies. Her eyeteeth protruded beyond her lower lip and her elderly body transmitted a sense of arcane power while a crimson seam running down the center of her face rapidly healed itself.

Noting that the number of demonic beings at the edge of Bachelors Grove Cemetery now far outnumbered the humans still there, Clayton saw Stephen Wentworth, lying on the ground. A quartet of unholy beings in their dingy, tattered robes attempted to sink their claws into the preacher's fallen body. However, their talons appeared to scrape against an invisible protective field.

Clayton's mind raced. The terrorized screams, the snarls of the attackers, the ground moving under their feet, all of this served to keep the confidence artist unbalanced, both physically and mentally. He felt the throbbing in his temples increase as did his desire to be a thousand miles away from this now-accursed place. With the situation so far beyond his control, running felt like the best option.

But where could he go if this chaos remained unchecked? How far would he be allowed to run?

Damn you, demons! Why did it take this horrific event to convince me that demons are real?

Then suddenly, Clayton looked down at his hands. They were tightly clasped together, solid, and unshaking.

He thought to himself, *DEMONS ARE REAL! I SEE THE EVIDENCE BEFORE ME! And if THEY are real ...*

He took a deep breath and stood as straight as he could. *I can work this grift, I know I can. But I'm gonna need some powerful help, and I'm going all the way to the top for it.*

The Right Reverend Josiah Clayton closed his eyes and bowed his head. Then a sincere, if halting, prayer of gratitude, for forgiveness, then for assistance, escaped his lips and his heart.

Immediately, his fear vanished. He smiled as cleansing tears flowed down his cheeks, and the burden of his pent-up guilt fell from his heart. Unashamedly, he lifted his head and opened his eyes in time to see the Moon pour its pure ivory light on them all.

If demons are real, then it makes sense YOU are REAL too, God ... MY God!

Rachel hissed. From the corner of his eye, Clayton saw

the woman's features become more animalistic, almost feral. "Silence, human!" Rachel spoke in a voice a couple of octaves lower than her true one. "Invoke His name once more, and I'll tear your soul into a billion pieces and watch each one drown in hellfire."

"Really, Rachel?" Clayton spoke clearly and with surprising conviction as he turned his gaze upwards, "Please forgive me for my part in this girl's corruption and for this twisted parody of righteousness. I sincerely repent my sins and place my wellbeing in Your hands."

Rachel howled in agony as Clayton's prayer ripped through her like a flaming sword. In response, her spine bent backwards, and she tore at her face with her talons. She undulated like a serpent, her scarlet eyes pouring their palpable hatred towards Clayton. The girl's fury increased as she realized her attempts to intimidate the pretend pastor proved to be for naught. She hurled obscenities and spat bloody phlegm at her opponent.

However, Clayton remained uncharacteristically calm. The bile and the winds seemed to avoid him as he faced Rachel with a serenity he'd never known before.

Clayton lifted his hands to the heavens and cried out, "Please bless this ground once more! Sanctify the land and grant eternal rest to its inhabitants! And please drive out the invaders to this world!"

He turned towards the creature that once had been Rachel. "While You're at it, I ask that You bless this young woman whose innocence I destroyed. Please forgive me my many transgressions, and grant the soul of Rachel Deeds peace and freedom from the demon inside her."

"Freedom?" Rachel's jaw unhinged, revealing two forked tongues wagging independently of each other. "She hated her mother, the repressive cow! So, I sat in the back of her mind, waiting for her to accept me. I didn't possess this shell, I *liberated* the girl."

Rachel chuckled. Her hair floated on the air like tentacles. "Now cease that miserable praying. Your God, if one exists, has forgotten you in your pathetic misery."

"Hardly!" Clayton stated with a conviction he'd never known before. "I now see you and your demons with brutal clarity. If you exist, and my words burn you, then how can a true God *not* exist?"

Filled with divinely-inspired confidence, Clayton filled his lungs to again lift his voice in prayer. Still, before he could utter another syllable, Rachel's slender hand clamped over his mouth and nose. Clayton struggled to regain his freedom, along with his ability to breathe, but Rachel's smoking, blistering flesh pressed tightly against his own skin.

"Can't pray if you can't inhale, can you?" Rachel's laughter drowned out the screams of the corrupted formerly-human shells as they danced in lewd celebration of their inevitable victory. With a sadistic grin, Rachel turned Clayton's face towards the unholy bacchanal.

Rachel's breath smelled like a warm grave as Clayton tried not to gag. "See that, Clayton? Soon, the vampires shall spread out from this humble acre until we claim all the lands surrounding Chicago. Then we shall move across Illinois and Indiana and soon, across the prairies as we feast upon the blood of the living and claim the bodies of those who remain."

Clayton felt Rachel's fingers weave through his hair. Suddenly, she jerked his head back and to the side hard enough that he was sure she'd snap his neckbone. He cringed as the demon's tongue slithered over the side of his throat, tracing a line of saliva over his jugular vein.

"But not all who die at our hands ... or fangs," Rachel whispered, "shall be reborn as one of us. Goodbye ... *'Uncle'* Josiah."

The Right Reverend Josiah Clayton felt Rachel's eyeteeth gently rake across the flesh covering his jugular vein. She inhaled sharply, savoring the rich aroma of fresh blood and fear.

His head held immobile, Clayton could just see the area beyond the cemetery gateway. Elaine Gale held Eloise high overhead, offering her sister's body to three demons who battled each other for the privilege of the woman's withered flesh.

And an empty spot remained where Stephen Wentworth once laid. *Not you too*, Clayton thought mournfully. He closed his eyes as a lack of oxygen turned the rest of his world to darkness.

Rachel's fangs pressed on Clayton's flesh and the Too-Late-A-Right-Reverend closed his eyes, preparing for his fate as he lifted his thoughts elsewhere. *I have been too weak and gave insincerely of what was expected of me, if I gave anything at all. I ask forgiveness from my victims and into Your hands, I commend my spirit.*

"Depart, demon!"

Rachel screeched as if drowning in a sea of acid in the moment that Stephen Wentworth seized her arm, pulling her claws free of Clayton's face. Flames burst to life where the man of God touched the possessed woman.

The Right Reverend Clayton immediately sucked in the sweetest lungful of air he could ever imagine.

Her arm smoking and useless from Wentworth's touch,

Rachel dropped Clayton, who fell to his knees. She gripped the spot where her assailant seized her and growled, "I'll tear you in half, rape your soul, violate everyone you ever –"

"No," Wentworth said calmly, with total conviction. "In the armor of our Creator, we are invincible." He knelt to help Clayton to his feet. "Join with me in prayer, my brother."

Clayton looked at Rachel. Despite the results of his own poor judgement, he looked past the demonic influence and now saw a beautiful, innocent girl, one that deserved salvation, just as he'd received the same.

Then, Clayton turned towards Wentworth, marveling at the steely gaze of a man who knew the power of true faith. At that moment, Clayton also realized the new-found depths of his own. "I would be grateful for the opportunity, my brother."

As one, the men lowered themselves to their knees and bowed their heads. Ignoring the chaos enveloping this tiny acre of creation, Clayton and Wentworth each spoke softly but with the power of a hurricane. "Our Father who art in Heaven, hallowed be Thy name ..."

Suddenly, a hush fell over the graveyard like a fresh blanket of snow in Winter and only their prayers could be heard: "Thy kingdom come, Thy will be done on Earth as it is in Heaven."

If they'd looked up, Clayton and Wentworth might have seen the moonlight shine like a spotlight on the acre of land that comprised the cemetery. As the men continued to pray, they could barely hear the flapping of angelic wings over their own powerful words. Clayton kept his eyes closed tightly, recalling Lot's wife and the penalty for peeking at things not meant to be seen by human beings.

The sound of swords slashing the night air preceded those of screaming demons as one by one, the damned fell before the might of their divine enemies. Clayton continued to whisper as rapturous tears rolled down his face. He felt Wentworth's elation as the other man's relieved laughter shook both his own body as well as Clayton's.

"Amen," both men said in unison.

Slowly, Clayton opened his eyes.

The landscape returned to a semblance of the sacred grounds it had been just an hour before. The gaggle of vampiric creatures raced for the sanctuary of their stone crypt. The edifice slowly sank back into the soil, barely allowing the robed monsters time to re-enter its safe, cold embrace.

However, not all the vampires returned to their sanctuary, Clayton noticed. He watched the snarling predators, all of whom used to be townspeople – parents, children, male and female alike – sprint into the woods while others raced down the pathway, disappearing into the night.

"Brother Clayton?"

Exhausted physically and emotionally, Clayton and Wentworth painfully rose to their feet and tilted their heads backwards, neither man ready for the sight that awaited them.

The woman they knew as Rachel Deeds now hovered several feet off the ground. Her drab clothing appeared to have been rewoven into gold and silver silks that waved gently in the cool breezes of the night. A look of tranquility now replaced her formerly twisted features as she smiled softly upon the gaping men below her.

"Yes," she said softly, "it's Rachel. I am saved, and I have you gentlemen to thank."

"I-I'm sorry," was all that Clayton could think to say. "Please forgive me for everything I did to you."

Rachel descended long enough to softly brush Clayton's cheek with a softly-glowing hand before rising into the air once more. "We are both redeemed." She indicated her new raiment. "But as you return to your life, I cannot to mine."

Wentworth shook his head. "Why not, young lady?"

"I was tethered to my mortal shell by a cord made of … well, call it a part of my soul." Rachel sighed. "This variety of vampirism is not like any other. I would have been forced to watch my body commit unimaginable atrocities until I either went mad … or I succumbed to its vile allure."

At that moment, the moonlight formed a tunnel of silver illumination around Rachel who found her attention drawn upwards. Her soft smile turned into a grin of bliss. She turned her face towards Clayton and Wentworth as her form ascended. "Bless you both as you have blessed me. Live righteously."

As if to punctuate her statement, the light surrounding Rachel grew brighter and brighter until the two men could no longer face it. They covered their eyes with their arms and still, the divine illumination penetrated their brains and the depths of their souls.

What felt like several minutes later, Clayton blinked the spots out of his eyesight. He slowly, carefully cast his eyes around the cemetery, savoring the unearthly silence. Then, one bird sang in the moonlight, followed by another.

"Did we succeed, Brother Clayton?" Wentworth blinked in confusion. "Everything seems as it was."

"Except for those poor souls now made undead." The Right Reverend Josiah Clayton smiled sincerely. "I think everything else has changed, though, hopefully for the better." He cast a wary glance over the grounds. "But only time will tell. Until then, can we give thanks?"

Wentworth nodded and lowered his head with Clayton who voiced his gratitude for his own salvation and for minimizing the loss of life this night. Once Clayton's prayer ended, Wentworth requested a blessing for all of Bachelors Grove Cemetery.

At that moment, the birds ceased singing and the Moon vanished behind a single dark cloud.

"I guess we've gotten all the blessings we can expect for one night," Wentworth concluded, rubbing his arm where the hair stood on end.

"We're alive and that's blessing enough for me." Clayton indicated the surviving townspeople with a tilt of his head. "Let's see to the living and get them home safely."

#

Josiah Clayton remained a guest in Stephen Wentworth's home for another week. During that time, he accompanied his host on his daily rounds, each man clutching his Bible tightly as they spoke with Wentworth's neighbors.

No one spoke of the incident at the cemetery, as if doing so might invoke the demons once more. But the Right Reverend Clayton never lacked for a friendly greeting from the townspeople of Bachelors Grove for the remainder of his stay. Clayton appreciated their grateful smiles.

Each morning, Clayton remembered to include Rachel in his newfound prayer routine.

Every night, Clayton dared to venture out after sundown. Many homes were now shuttered as if expecting a storm. The braver households simply pulled their curtains shut, nervous eyes peering outside between the gaps in the fabric.

And at the Gale sisters' home, Clayton swore he saw two identical silhouettes on the curtains each night. The sisters' wicked laughter chilled the man's soul as his pace took him rapidly to the far side of the street.

But seven mornings after Rachel's ascension, Clayton climbed onto his buckboard, promising to visit his family's ranch. "Perhaps I am to be the prodigal son. If I am to make amends, let it start at home."

"I'm sure they will be as proud of you as I am for accepting your faults and working to change them." Wentworth ran a hand through his hair, the roots of which now showed a hint of pure white. "I know you've done more than you've told me, but that's between you and God. All I know is if you weren't a good man before, you certainly may be one now."

Clayton shrugged. "I don't know about that, my friend. But I plan to also throw myself at the mercy of Mrs. Deeds, and then at the local sheriff." He grinned. "Prison now holds no terror for me since I gazed into the depths of Hell itself. Besides, if I can help reach one soul in there, then perhaps that's where the Lord intended me."

Wentworth chuckled. "He *does* work in mysterious ways, I've read." The preacher bit his lower lip. "But until you get there …?"

"I shall fear no evil," Clayton promised. "And if Satan himself should bar my way, I'll show the old trickster what the grift is truly about." The man's expression turned serious. "Now, it's personal and all I can tell you is pray for the Devil. He's going to need all the help he can get."

"I'd say Ol' Scratch himself doesn't stand a chance." Wentworth shook Clayton's hand one last time. "Thank you for reassuring me of my faith."

Clayton grinned. "And thank you for helping me locate my own. If I get to travel this way again, I promise to visit. Good day, Brother Wentworth."

"Safe travels, Brother Clayton," Wentworth wished his

friend. Clayton's horse pulled the wagon down the street and onto the lane that passed the cemetery.

Refusing to even glance through the iron gates, or to acknowledge the sound of bubbling from the nearby pond, Josiah Clayton rode towards the southwest, towards the rest of his new life.

SACRIFICES

By

Brian K. Morris

Reginald Kohlman refused to live an ordinary life. This would be a good thing if only Reginald wasn't such a pain in the ass.

Every morning at 8:15, his doting mother, Edna, trimmed her son's ponytail, guaranteeing that no single strand of his blonde mane would be closer to the ground than another. Reginald even demanded that his mother use a carpenter's level to ensure the equal status of each hair before tying it into a ponytail.

His father, Robert, left for work every morning, confident that his spouse could keep up with their sole offspring's numerous demands. When Reginald was born thirty-two years ago, the couple knew their only son would become a celebrity, probably curing cancer, or writing music that would leave the angels smashing their harps in tearful envy.

But once Reginald slipped on his wire-rimmed glasses for the day, the blue eyes behind those lenses saw nothing but what pleased the only child of Edna and Robert. And those doting parents would have life happen no other way.

"Mother," Reginald chastised his mater at the breakfast table, a bite of cheese pizza pushed back into the corner of his mouth, "could you stop humming? I've got to review this comic book online in an hour? Jay-*zus*, how am I supposed to make my vlog deadlines with all these interruptions?"

Reginald's rebuke, like most of his statements, issued forth with machine gun rapidity, slammed against Edna's maternal values. "Sorry, son." Duly admonished, Reginald's mother placed the last plate into the dishwasher. She waited for her son to finish his breakfast before switching it on because the machine could be heard over his favorite cartoon, which had to be listened to at a specific volume, according to Reginald, to be appropriately appreciated.

One day last month, Edna mentioned to a friend from church about her son's unique demands for an ordered life. *His* ordered life, a life of modest challenges, and maximum expectations which continually yielded minimal rewards.

The friend smiled unsympathetically. "I think you didn't

hug that boy enough when he was a kid, or you hugged him too much."

Mother contemplated her son's daily routine, writing comic book reviews for an entertainment video blog that paid in something called "exposure." She wasn't certain when, or how, this lucre could be converted into bill and rent-paying cash, but whatever Reginald wanted was Reginald's to expect. Oh, and Edna never spoke to that so-called friend ever again.

After uploading his newest review to his website, Reginald went to work on another Facebook post, promoting his appearance at the Rawhide City Comic Con. *Come see the latest issue,* he posted, *of my great new comic book,* Captain Heroic. *I will also read my favorite reviews from my website all weekend. Look for the coolest guy you know, the man with the narrow waistline and the biggest smile.*

Reginald grinned. If his fans were lucky, they might be treated to his rendition of the Goku Vs. Superman Rap Battle.

The next day at the convention, Reginald dropped a fistful of candy across the purple bedsheet that adorned his folding table. Then, Reginald placed all seven issues of his self-published comic book onto his homemade stands, making certain that the weight of each magazine didn't overwhelm the strength of the electrician's tape holding the crudely-shaped cardboard easels together.

Now that the sales area met his standards of perfection, Reginald went behind the table and reassured himself that his properly-displayed series of *Captain Heroic*s lay ready for his annual assault on the editors from the major publishers. Just as he had done for the last eight years running, Reginald vowed on his Facebook page that he would emerge from this show as a full-fledged employee of one of those companies.

Reginald never bought anything from those guys, but he read the comps his local comic shop gave him for a mention in his review blog.

For eight years, Reginald Kohlman purchased booth space at the Rawhide City Comic Con's Artists Alley to have a base of operations at this show. He sold enough comics to pay for a quarter of his table on a good year, and to be the center of attention for three days.

His labors done, Reginald dropped onto his folding chair and scanned his Instagram page on his phone. He grinned when three of his followers "loved" yesterday's post.

"How's it going, guy?"

Reginald aimed his sternest glare at the voice, ready to deliver a scathing rebuke for interrupting this precious online time before the fanboy attendees sucked up all the free wi-fi. Instead, something inside told Reginald to be polite just long enough to appear professional. After all, it didn't pay to annoy anyone who might be useful one day.

"I'm P. Keith Barnett, novelist" the man said with a smile, extending his hand. "I guess I'm your next-door neighbor."

The man appeared to be close to retirement age, although his silver hair was thick and wavy in a rockstar way that made Reginald gag mentally. The man wore a three-piece charcoal gray suit as well as a pair of black shoes so well-shined that Reginald saw his reflection in them.

Reginald cautiously offered his own hand, allowing it to be firmly seized as his fingers went limp. After all, an overly-muscular hand fared poorly at video games.

Barnett glanced over Reginald's offerings. "I see you write comics. I used to do that long ago."

Mistaking courtesy for genuine interest, Reginald forced a smile onto his lips. "Why did you stop? No money?"

Chuckling as he spread a bright blue cover over his table, Barnett said, "Nope. In the mid-Eighties, a whole bunch of distributors got in over their heads, and I lost my editorial accounts. However, with the help of a friendly soul, I got into novels, and the field's been very kind to me."

"So, what did you write? Would I have heard of them?"

Barnett tilted his head back and laughed. "Depends on when you started reading comics." He then rattled off over a dozen best-selling characters that Reginald would have given a kidney to write. In fact, he followed most of those titles in the hopes of one day seeing his writing credit on the cover.

"No joke?" Reginald grabbed the first issue of *Captain Heroic* and dropped it on Barnett's table. "Would you mind reading my comic and tell me what you think?" He added with a smirk. "I mean as long as you aren't doing anything important."

Barnett nodded and continued to set up his display. The man created nine piles of books, each one comprised of a specific title, before setting up a sign with his name and credits boldly displayed on its front, as well as a small plastic holder filled with his business cards. Then, Barnett unfolded his metal chair and sat down, dropping a half-dozen pens from his jacket pocket onto the table, ready to autograph.

Reginald pushed the first issue of his comic book onto the center of Barnett's table, directly in front of the author. "Um, if you don't mind. Maybe before the doors open and the customers block my table?"

The corner of Barnett's mouth rose slightly as he picked up the comic. Reginald bristled at Barnett's impassive expression. He felt the man should be touched by the privilege of reading an issue for free.

After a couple of minutes, Barnett stopped reading and commenced scanning the pages, flipping them one after another. Then, he handed the comic back to Reginald with a polite smile.

"So whatcha think?" Reginald braced himself for the inevitable shower of praise. Surely the validation from a man who had so many "real" books in print could do nothing but help sales. Maybe the novelist would ask to do a review on Goodreads. Yeah, Reginald didn't really know what Goodreads did, but he knew it was impressive if you read real books, which he didn't.

Barnett tapped his chin with his index finger, pondering his next remark. "Well, first, thanks for letting me see this.

The art's pretty good, even if everyone's pretty much just standing around, talking. I could wish for a little more action, something more visual. Even the body language is a little bit too calm for me. The artist could take a few lessons from, say, Jack Kirby."

"Yeah, I think my mom owns one of his vacuum cleaners." Reginald grimaced. "Okay. What else?"

"Well," Barnett continued, "you don't list your name or anyone else who collaborated on this book. I mean this comic book is your calling card, so in case you use it to get some freelance work, you want folks to know who's responsible, right?"

"Everyone knows it's mine." Reginald crossed his arms and frowned. "I mean I put my name all over my Kickstarter page as well as my personal Facebook and Twitter accounts."

"But what if they don't follow you on social media? How will they know then?"

Reginald fumed silently. How could anyone not know him from his numerous posts on fifteen prominent websites devoted to classic anime? "I suppose there's more?"

"I could go on, but I hate to nitpick." Barnett handed

Reginald his business card. "I think you're off to a fine start. Good luck this weekend."

Reginald stared at the card as if he was asked to examine a stool sample. Barnett noticed the writer's pained expression. "Um, do you have a card for my files?" When Reginald shook his head, Barnett asked, "You don't have business cards? I mean there's no mention of your e-mail or website inside your comic. Did you leave them at home?"

"No." Reginald inhaled sharply. "I think having candy on my table draws more customers than a scrap of cardboard. I mean where the heck are your treats?" *Stop picking on my display, old man*, Reginald thought, *because you've got seven more issues to publish to catch up with me.*

Barnett smiled. "Different strokes. Anyway, good luck."

At the top of the hour, the promoter gave a brief speech, welcoming the attendees to the Rawhide City Comic Con. Then, the doors opened, and the inrush of people reminded the wide-eyed front line of vendors of the Running of the Bulls.

Several cosplayers held up their badges to prove they paid their admission fee. Once inside, they tucked the laminated squares into the depths of their costume in order

253

to remain as on-model as possible. At one entryway, a uniformed security guard examined an all-too-realistic broadsword, ignoring the owner's protests.

A dozen men and woman desperately clutched their dark leather portfolio cases. Each nervous potential comics professional pulled out their program book and checked out the consecutively numbered banners overhead. Stars danced in their eyes as they silently prayed for a job offer. Meanwhile, dozens of men and women swiftly swarmed the auditorium, scanning the rows and rows of dealers for the latest in geek-related wares, licensed or otherwise.

By the time the crowd filtered through the aisles to Artists Alley, P. Keith Barnett was on his feet, smile affixed to his lips, ready to greet his potential customers.

Beside him, Reginald Kohlman looked up from his phone, having tweeted news of his latest Pokémon Go acquisition. He snorted derisively at his neighbor. *Wotta amateur.*

Over the next couple of hours, Reginald noticed the easy charm the older man exuded towards his customers and the book piles shrinking on Barnett's table. He then looked down at his comics, still on their makeshift displays, their numbers minimally diminished. However, most of his candy had vanished.

Barnett gave two-sentence pitch for each of his books to a couple, each of whom wore matching shirts, eyewear, and cloaks. They nodded as he concluded each two-sentence routine and waited for their reaction as befitted any good showman.

"Jay-*zus*, I've been listening to his stale rap all morning, over and over and over." Reginald complained to his other neighbor, a woman who sold handmade "magic wands." "Doesn't he know how annoying that is? He should change that up, if just for my sake."

Reginald waited for the woman to reply, but instead, she concentrated on conversing with her customer, a middle-aged woman dressed like a Hogwarts student.

"Excuse me, but I asked you a question."

The vendor looked up and whispered an apology to her customer from the side of her mouth before replying to Reginald with an edge in her voice, "You might also notice that he's selling a lot, too. Perhaps you could take some lessons from him."

"Start with some courtesy," the customer suggested before she joined the vendor in ignoring Reginald.

"Mm-mm. You're gonna be nicer to me when I'm working for one of the big comic book publishers." Reginald said, his brow furrowed, and a finger placed on the tip of his chin, just like they did on television when pondering an important idea. He glanced around and said, "Mm-mm," even more loudly.

Barnett returned the newest buyer's credit card just autographing his latest book.

"Mm-mm," Reginald stated with conviction. He contemplated repeating his "Mm-mm" until his phone's timer buzzed in his back pocket. Reginald checked the screen, then bolted from his booth, four non-consecutive issues of his comics in his hand.

Two panels and three portfolio reviews later, Reginald returned to his booth, looking as if someone spoiled a newly-released film for him. Without looking at his neighbors on the other side of his table, he asked Barnett, "What sold?"

Barnett drank deeply from his water bottle. Smiling softly, he stated, "I've had to restock a couple of times. In fact, I'm almost out of –"

"I didn't mean *you*." Reginald shook his head so his pony tail wouldn't get caught between his back and the top of the folding chair, just as he'd practiced for months. "I meant *my* stuff."

"You didn't ask me to watch your table, sorry. Just the same, I don't think anyone stole anything." Barnett replaced the cap on his water bottle. "I can't swear to that. I've been pretty busy."

"Yeah," Reginald stated with no small amount of annoyance. "I noticed." He pondered Barnett's table for a moment. "So, what could I do to sell more comics?"

"Just off the top of my head, I'd drop a few dollars and make my displays a little slicker. I haven't been able to watch your pitch but −"

Reginald frowned deeply. "People love my displays. They stand out. They're gonna make me an overnight sensation."

Barnett smiled. "You have time."

"I don't want to wait." Reginald contemplated the concept of turning forty while still living with his parents and shivered, but not with delight.

"Don't get impatient, Reginald. It took me a few decades to become an 'overnight sensation.' If you apply yourself, it'll happen." Barnett snapped his fingers. "Oh, I overheard you telling someone you were applying for a gig with the big boys. Did you get any traction?"

Reginald's expression turned sour. "Yeah, I saw them. Seven editors in all."

Grinning, Barnett asked, "You did well, I take it.?

"No!" Reginald took a deep breath. "No, I didn't."

"What did they say?"

Reginald looked down at his shoes, speaking quickly, "They didn't see my credits, too many talking heads." While Barnett said that he didn't want to nitpick the *Captain Heroic*s to death, those seven editors never showed a second's hesitation to rip the stories to shreds. On the other hand, four of those editors asked for his artist's contact information. Reginald sighed.

Barnett chuckled as he checked his list of books to confirm the correct number of sales made so far. "Well, I mentor a lot of people. If you have any questions, I'll either try to answer them or steer you to someone who can."

"You will?"

"Sure." Barnett chuckled. "A lot of people gave me useful information on my way up. The least I can do is share with the next generation." He smiled. "My e-mail's on the card."

Reginald patted his pocket, confirming the business card was still there. "So, tell me, what's the most important part of this job? Writing or promotion?"

Without hesitation, Barnett stated with all due seriousness, "Neither. In the end, it's all about sacrifice. What are you willing to give up to get ahead?"

"I understand," Reginald lied. "What did you give up?

"Television. Video games. People who drained my time like a vampire drank blood." Barnett's voice grew even more grim. "There are people who don't want to see you succeed, Reginald. Trust me on this. They think you are stealing their happiness if you move up in life. Don't be afraid to leave people behind."

"Mm-mm." However, Reginald's mind whirled with this new information. "So where are you going to be next?"

Pulling out his phone, Barnett opened his calendar. "It looks like three weeks from now, I'll be in Indianapolis for Acceller XVIII." Barnett pronounced the convention's name as it was intended, *Accelerate-Teen*. "It's a science fiction show that does right by me."

"Send me the promoter's name," Reginald commanded

rapidly. Then, he softened his tone. "I wouldn't mind checking that one out. My stuff's pretty sci-fi."

Barnett bit his tongue. "Can't hurt to try." Then, he returned his attention to his customers. "Hi, folks. My name's Keith. What do you like to read?"

"Mm-mm," Reginald said, not caring if anyone heard.

"Mister Drake? Have any tables left for that Acceller con?

"Good. My name's Reginald Kohlman.

"Kohlman.

"Reginald Kohlman. I write and publish comics that are kinda sci-fi. Anyway, I'd like a table for the show.

"*That* much? Jay-*zus*, that's a lot.

"No, I'll take it.

"However, I gotta be next to P. Keith Barnett. He and I are tight, you know."

Three weeks later, the doors opened at the eighteenth Acceller Convention. P. Kevin Barnett rose to greet the onslaught of attendees. As one of the guests of honor, the front of Barnett's table filled immediately with fans, eager to see his latest works.

"Make way. Coming through."

Reginald Kohlman pulled his cart through the crowd, cutting through the throng that had assembled in front of Barnett's table. "Hi, Barney!" He turned towards the people congregating in front of Barnett's display and called out, "Hey, this guy's good. He's got this great rap. Make sure you hear the one with the punchline about the Cthulhu gods."

Reginald grinned at Barnett who could only stare with surprise at his neighbor's presence, to say nothing of his nerve.

The younger writer pulled his comics from the depths of his well-worn bootleg Naruto backpack, along with the makeshift easels, most of which were crushed from the weight of the magazines dropped on top of them at the conclusion of the last show.

"Hey, Barney!" Reginald called out. "Got any duct tape? Gotta shore up my stands."

Barnett sighed. He smiled at the attractive young woman holding one of his books in her long, delicate hands. "Excuse me." He turned to Reginald. "No, sorry. I don't carry any duct tape with me." The question answered, Barnett returned his attention to his potential customer.

"Hey!" Reginald called out at Barnett. "I wasn't done talking to you. Do you have an extension cord?"

"I'm sorry, but –"

As Barnett turned to address his neighbor, Reginald saw a pack of what appeared to be Klingons, then turned his back on the author and began dancing what appeared to be the Macarena.

Barnett sighed. He smiled at his customer, ready to give his apology for allowing himself to be distracted. Unfortunately, the woman already vacated her space at the table, placing the book she'd once favored on the appropriate pile. Barnett sighed once more and unscrewed the cap on his water bottle. He glanced over towards Reginald who stood on his chair, still dancing and grinning as he noticed the stares he attracted while not paying any attention to their snickering.

Reginald glanced down towards Barnett. "You never did answer my question."

Barnett shrugged, turning his attention back to the fresh pack of fans that found their way to his table. By this time, a couple of people strolled up to Reginald's display. One young man who wore a set of horn-rimmed glasses and a bootleg Bat-emblem t-shirt, thumbed through the third issue of *Captain Heroic*.

"Good stuff, huh?" Reginald bounced off the chair and proceeded to jabber rapidly at his customer. In the space of twenty seconds, the wannabe Gothamite found himself treated to the plot of each issue of *Captain Heroic* as well as the psychological background of each of the major protagonists and all the villains, the ending of every other issue, to say nothing of the quality of the series and how much Reginald's autograph would be worth someday.

After finally taking a breath, Reginald turned towards his neighbor and what he saw immediately dismissed any thoughts of selling or attracting attention to himself.

Standing in front of Barnett's table was a young woman who appeared to be in her early twenties. Her long hair fell down to her shoulder blades like a scarlet waterfall and a tight blue knit dress hugged her full curves. Barnett smiled softly at the lady who allowed her Dirty Pair backpack to rest at her feet.

With her arms crossed and her green eyes staring at the older writer from over her glasses, the woman gave the impression of being a school teacher from some '80s music video. When Barnett stopped talking for a moment and glanced at her, the woman's face lit up with the brightest smile Reginald had seen outside of a toothpaste commercial.

Without another word to the potential purchaser of his comic books, Reginald leaped behind Barnett's table. He nudged the older writer backwards to insert himself into the woman's exclusive field of sight. "Hi, I'm Reginald Kohlman and I publish *Captain Heroic*."

The woman's eyes narrowed for a moment. Then, with a gentle rise of the corners of her perfect lips, she said softly, "Well, good for you. But, I was talking to Mr. Barnett, if you don't mind."

"I have some books you might be interested in. They're better than books. If books were any good, then I'd write some. So, what's your name?"

The woman attempted to re-establish eye contact with Barnett, but Reginald wasn't having that. He moved to block her view of her intended target.

"My name is Mary Lou Brady," she stated with a sigh. "I'm sure I'll make it over to your area later."

Leaning across the table and reaching for Mary Lou's

arm, Reginald grinned. "Why wait? Are you a reporter? You need to interview me. My hair is very visual."

"What I am," the woman stated firmly, "is annoyed by your rudeness, *Mister* Kohlman. Now, I'd like to continue to speak to Keith. I was about to add 'if you don't mind,' *but* that doesn't make any difference."

Reginald felt Barnett's hands on his shoulders just before being guided back to his own sales space.

"You need to learn some manners, young man," Barnett whispered into Reginald's ear.

"But, I didn't do anything," Reginald protested.

However, Barnett wasn't having any of Reginald's nonsense any more than the young woman. "You are being quite rude, young man. If you try to poach any of my customers or ruin my pitches again, I will have a word with the promoters about you. Do you understand?"

Reginald nodded quickly, adding a scowl of silent protest, so Barnett released him. The younger writer blinked back tears of frustration and looked over to his neighbor's booth. The smile already returned to Barnett's face as he approached Mary Lou whose face brightened in return.

She is pretty, Reginald admitted to himself. Suddenly,

he attempted to recall the last time he went on a date and could only come up with his senior prom from fourteen years ago. He asked all the cheerleading squad, as well as most of the other attractive girls in school, to be his date and even offered to pay for their fuel if they picked him up on time. Oddly enough, all of them declined the honor.

Several, in fact, promised to tell their boyfriends, offering their maidenly virtue in exchange for the opportunity to hear the news of Reginald's appearance at an emergency room of their choosing.

Reginald certainly showed those stuck-up hos when he attended his senior prom dressed like Ash – and not that Bruce Campbell-pretender's version, but the real one from Pokémon – with his mother on his arm.

But now, Reginald studied the curves of the young woman who appeared to hang onto Barnett's every word. A peculiar feeling washed over the comics writer, making him feel every day of his thirty-two years.

Loneliness.

Now forlorn, Reginald replaced the comic book on his makeshift stand, and as a result, the old duct tape gave way and the display collapsed to the table. At this moment, Reginald recalled his high school English classes and the mention of "metaphor."

On the other hand, enough adhesive remained on the tape to cling to the comic's cover and would tear a small hole in it when it was removed. But Reginald didn't care. All he saw was *his* Mary Lou spending time with someone else.

What does that old man have that I don't? Other than sales and consistent traffic and a following, that is? Didn't she see my ponytail?

Reginald edged closer to Barnett's table. Over the din of the convention, he could just hear the older writer's words.

"I'm constantly asked what's the most important part about writing. Is it grammar? Is it promotion? Is it the cover artwork?" He gave Mary Lou time to consider the questions and then to shake her lovely head, leaving Barnett to continue. "It's sacrifice."

"Sacrifice?" Mary Lou shifted her weight from one foot to the other. "You mentioned that in your lectures at my school. However, I'm not sure what you're talking about."

Barnett swept his hand over his display of novels. "I gave up television and a lot of my social life to produce so much work. I also gave up many distractions to learn more about the current state of book publishing. That meant a lot

267

of hours in a library. I still cruise the internet, looking for new data on writing, publishing, and promotion." He added with a wide-eyed grin, "I also make the occasional virgin sacrifices to the dark lords who live under the ocean. However, to balance out my karma, I gladly give instruction to up-and-comers, just like I used to be."

Mary Lou laughed and to Reginald, it sounded like poetry. He never knew a time when he'd wanted a specific woman the way he did this one. Not a living woman, as opposed to someone he found in a comic book or cartoon.

"Thank you," Mary Lou said with the brightest teeth Reginald had ever seen. "I look forward to talking to you at length about your ... sacrifices, Keith." She quickly strode behind Barnett's table to give the man a tight hug which the writer returned warmly.

As their hands moved up and down each other's backs, Reginald seethed with jealousy. He eyed the shrinking stacks of the author's works and the satisfied expression on Mary Lou's sweet face and decided *What you have, Barnett, I want for myself, whatever it takes! WHATEVER!*

Reginald cast an unpleasant smile towards Barnett. *I look forward to studying with you too.*

#

Later that night, in his hotel room, P. Kevin Barnett saved the latest of his writings to the cloud when Facebook Messenger dinged for his attention.

Barnett picked up his phone and tapped the screen to life. He waited for the Messenger window to open, hoping it was Landry Hills, one of his favorite show promoters, with final information on his travel itinerary. Instead, what Barnett read made his ulcer flare.

Reginald Kohlman: YOU THERE?

Reginald Kohlman: YOU THERE?

"Nope, I'm not," Barnett whispered to the phone as he closed the window. Eight hours' worth of the younger man's jumping about, non-stop chatter, incessant questions, and outright rudeness was enough for one day.

Just before Barnett could toss his phone onto the bed, it rang. He usually didn't pick up calls from unknown numbers, but something told him it could be Mary Lou Brady. His index finger slid across the faceplate and he pulled the device to his ear. "Hello?"

"Hey, Barney," came the all-too cheerful voice that Barnett welcomed hearing as much as he might the sound of a dentist's drill. "Got some time?"

"Not really," Barnett said, his fingers crossed. "Just wanting to unwind after a long day with some writing."

"Yeah, must be tough selling so many books." Reginald didn't wait for Barnett to reply. "Listen, I didn't get a room for the night, and I don't feel like sleeping at a truck stop. Can I crash with you?"

The thought of sharing a living space and a night without a respite from Reginald's voice sent icy fear on a stroll up and down Barnett's spine. "Sorry. Only a single bed here."

Hearing Reginald's sigh of disappointment brought a smile to Barnett's face which grew as he said, "So, I guess I'll see you tom–"

"Listen, I heard you talk about getting some real editing on your work. Can I get you to read my comic scripts and tell me what I need to know? I mean you've been doing this long enough that you might have learned something I didn't, right?"

Barnett listened thoughtfully. He knew the kid was playing on his ego, but maybe, just maybe, it wouldn't hurt to give the guy some helpful advice. "I could."

Immediately, Barnett's phone emitted a tone that

informed him that a new file entered his message queue. Before he could tilt the phone to see who sent it, Reginald said, "You can get that done by tomorrow, okay? I'm going to get some sleep."

The phone went dead in Barnett's hand. He pressed the message icon and began to read ... and read ... and read ...

#

Reginald sat behind his table, refreshed from a full night's sleep at the truck stop. Barnett approached, sipping at his coffee from a travel mug adorned with the cover of his latest book.

Skipping any greeting, Reginald cried out cheerfully, "Go ahead. Let me have it. How brilliant were my scripts?"

Barnett slowly placed the cup on his table. "First of all, I left you some comments in a private message. But, you have too many consecutive pages of the same two characters, just standing and talking to each other. You need to have them move, gesture, change their location, do something that's visually interesting. And have them show some emotion, for Heaven's sake."

Reginald's smile fled his lips, and his expression turned dark. "But it's great dialog. Sounds natural, right?"

"Too natural, if anything," Barnett stated. "You clearly love your characters and how they interact. However, you do little to advance the plot or illuminate anyone's character. You might as well have them discuss a grocery list. In addition, your grammar is awful. Maybe if you worked on your conversational grammar, your written prose would improve."

"I know all that," Reginald said impatiently. "Jay-*zus*! That's just what the pro editors told me. I wanted something new."

"Also," Barnett continued, "who writes to their artist in future tense? If you remove the passive verbs from your dialog, you'll save –"

"ALRIGHT!" Reginald shouted. "Wow, what a crank."

Before Barnett could reply to Reginald's rudeness, the dealers room doors swung inward and the first wave of the day's customers entered. Barnett's expression brightened at seeing Mary Lou Brady waving as she approached his table.

"Hey, Mary Lou!" Reginald shouted as he sprang from his chair. He rounded the table and greeted her with a huge hug that made one of her vertebrae crack in protest.

"Hi," she replied, her eyes still on Barnett who smiled

sympathetically and shrugged helplessly.

"I got an extra chair for you," Reginald stated as he attempted to guide her steps towards his table.

Mary Lou turned her most withering glare on Reginald and shrugged hard enough to dislodge his arm. "Thank you, but I've been invited to sit with Mr. Barnett." With that, she resumed her trek towards the older writer's table.

Barnett smiled warmly at Mary Lou, then at the new group of attendees that assembled before his table, each person examining copies of his many novels.

As Mary Lou studied Barnett while he peddled his wares, she became aware of a presence at her shoulder. Without looking back, she said dryly, "Reginald, you do realize you're invading my personal space."

"I didn't think you'd mind," Reginald whispered.

"You didn't think, period," Mary Lou countered. "Back up and stay behind your table. That way, you might be able to keep something you could use later."

Chuckling, Reginald continued to whisper, "So why do you keep trying to get close to him?"

"Same reason you are, little man." Mary Lou had a strange, half-lidded look that left Reginald blinking in confusion. "Keith's got a lot of knowledge that he's willing to share, and not just about writing."

She's calling him "Keith?" Reginald thought. "Yeah, I noticed too," the man had to admit. "That's why I checked Barnett's website for his convention schedule. I called and asked all of the promoters to place me next to Barney."

"Clever boy." Mary Lou stroked her chin thoughtfully. "You know, he's looking for a writing intern, if you will, someone he'll train personally." She studied Reginald for a moment. "You knew that, right?"

"Yeah, I knew that," Reginald said too hastily to convince Mary Lou that he spoke the truth. A look into her emerald eyes informed the writer that she'd never buy into any of his lies, mostly the ones he told himself.

As this thought crossed Reginald's mind, he felt a familiar, firm grip on his shoulder.

"Is he bothering you again?" Barnett asked Mary Lou. Any hint of the man's kindly nature yielded to his annoyance with Reginald. "I can talk to the promoter and have this guy removed."

Mary Lou looked at Reginald and saw an unfamiliar fear in his eyes. "No. Why cause a scene?" She growled to the younger man, "Go back to your chair, please."

Barnett released Reginald, giving him a small shove in doing so. His gaze dropped to the floor as he backed towards his chair.

It wasn't until Barnett assumed his usual professional, friendly tones with a new customer that Reginald dared look up again. For once, he was grateful to be ignored as both Barnett and Mary Lou kept their backs to him.

But in surveying Mary Lou, Reginald's appreciation for her back, and related body parts, grew. He reluctantly pulled his gaze from the woman to the relative comfort of checking his cell phone.

Let's look at Barnett's edit, Reginald thought as he opened the e-mail. The time stamp verified that it was sent at a very late hour the night before. *He really went to some trouble,* Reginald thought, humbled for a moment. *Just for me.* A minute's worth of study inspired Reginald to say, "Mm-mm."

These edits are ... they're awesome. Reginald's finger slid across the screen, scrolling the documents which he read eagerly. Each correction dropped the word count, strengthened the narrative, provided more character, and foreshadowed events happening at the end of each story.

Reginald found himself impressed with the thoroughness of the edit and follow-up comments.

Barnett appeared confident as he pitched his books to the people who listened attentively. More than half of the time while Reginald observed Barnett, the man made a sale. Even when he didn't, he often handed the attendee a business card and thanked them for their time.

As if being so together wasn't enough to make Reginald jealous, Mary Lou ignored him to study the older man with fascination. She rested a small notepad on her well-shaped knee and scribbled line after line of her observations for later review.

Poise, competence, and a groupie … Reginald ground his teeth together as a plan formed in his mind.

# # #

Two Saturdays later, Reginald Kohlman pulled his cart to his table. Taking a page from P. Keith Barnett's playbook, Reginald arrived an hour early, giving him time to execute a leisurely set-up of his seven comic books.

Reginald observed that his neighbors arrived much earlier than him as evidenced by the near-completion of their displays. He stopped, read the names on their banners, frowned, then sprinted back towards the registration desk.

A retired mailman wearing a special con t-shirt with the convention's logo screen-printed on the front and the word "VOLUNTEER" on the back handed a lanyard to a young woman on the other side of the counter. He smiled sweetly and thanked the tattooed jewelry vendor for her patience with the glacier slowness of the computer's registration system.

The woman barely turned to leave when Reginald elbowed past her to confront the volunteer. "Excuse me," the writer growled, "but you seem to have made a mistake with my seating." Reginald frowned at the elder man's thick waves of silver hair and neatly-trimmed eyebrows.

"Kohlman, right?" The volunteer consulted his computer screen and then a print-out to confirm. "Um, I gave you the correct booth number, didn't I? You did see your name taped to the top of the table, right?"

"Yeah, I did." Reginald took a deep breath, trying to calm himself. "But, I specifically asked to be seated next to P. Keith Barnett."

"Ah, yes." The older man gnawed his lower lip nervously. "I'm aware of that. My son's the promoter, and he told me about you."

"Yippie-ti-yay for nepotism," Reginald snarled, his fists pressed onto the tabletop in front of the volunteer. "Well, he's not where he's supposed to be, which is at the table beside mine."

"There's been no mistake."

Reginald turned to see Mary Lou Brady. She stood before the writer in a bright blue power suit with matching glasses, shirt and necktie. Her initials adorned the leather of her leather shoulder bag, just as Reginald's mother embroidered her son's name inside all his clothing.

Mary Lou turned to the volunteer, smiling brightly. "Hi, I'm here to pick up Mr. Barnett's guest package. He's already setting up." Her smile dimmed as she turned towards Reginald. "Good morning, Mr. Kohlman. You see, as P. Keith Barnett's new assistant, I took the liberty of calling every promoter on the tour to request that your table not be placed next to his." Her smile made a brief reappearance. "As per Mr. Barnett's wishes."

"You can't do that!" Reginald's face flushed and his reserve burned fast and hot, just like a fuse. "Not any more. I don't consent, so there."

Enjoying Reginald's visible discomfort, Mary Lou smiled brilliantly once more. "True. I can't do it anymore only because I've run out of promoters to call." She sighed. "I honestly wish it hadn't come to this, but you left us no choice."

Reginald's lower lip quivered. "But I've got a reputation. I've published six more comics than most people my age. Than most people, period."

"Then, perhaps your reputation isn't as good as Mr. Barnett's, who's getting his way." Mary Lou smiled softly. "Actually, you've published seven more comics than a lot of fans. Most wannabe publishers never leave the talking-about-it phase," Mary Lou corrected. "You should take pride in that."

"I *am* proud of what I've done." Mary Lou's scalpel-sharp gaze, along with her sincere assessment of his accomplishments, left Reginald feeling very, very small. "I really am," he added with less confidence.

"You're a good kid, even if you take advantage of Keith Barnett a little too much," Mary Lou stated softly. "You just need to learn about courtesy and professionalism. Now, if you'll excuse me." With that, she blew the volunteer a kiss and walked into the heart of the dealers room, towards Barnett's table.

Reginald strolled back to his space, his hands crammed

into his jeans pockets with his morale dragging along behind him. He looked up occasionally to study the expressions of the convention attendees and the vendors behind the tables. Reginald noted their smiles, the warmth of their conversations, the pleasure each took from the other. He sighed every time he saw two people call out each other's names just prior to a tight embrace.

When was the last time someone called out my name, like they were happy to see me? Reginald mused as he dropped onto his folding chair. *When did I ever get a hug that I didn't initiate? More importantly, why haven't I gotten these things?*

Reginald knew the answer to his own questions before he asked them. He bit his lip and took a hard look at the person he'd become over the years.

Am I that rude? Am I too wrapped up in myself? Too ambitious? Too ungrateful? Do I really take advantage of others?

But worse, he looked at himself through Mary Lou Brady's eyes and found the view quite unpleasant indeed. *Should I change? Can I?*

# # #

Barnett called it "singing for his supper," his usual offer to host or appear on a panel. He knew many conventions wanted content for their attendees. Thus, Barnett didn't mind straying from his table for an hour to moderate a panel. It didn't hurt that someone as charming as Mary Lou Brady would watch his table for him.

The path to the auditorium led Barnett past Reginald Kohlman's table. Deciding to take the higher path and keep his karma in the positive, Barnett steeled his resolve to politely greet the younger writer on his way to the panel.

Barnett approached Kohlman's space, noticing that no one sat behind the table. The dealers on either side of the empty booth appeared to be somewhat relieved, casting the occasional smile at the empty chair between then.

Shrugging, Barnett stepped up his pace to get to his appointment with the fans. He approached the open entrance to the auditorium, but stopped in the doorway. Usually, the air would be thick with the sound of people shuffling down the rows to find their seats amidst the general hubbub of conversation.

However, instead of the attendees' white noise, Barnett heard only one sound, a specific amplified voice which rested in his ears like hot razor blades.

Barnett looked up to the stage at the far end of the auditorium and standing behind the podium was Reginald Kohlman. The man's smile shone brighter than the lights above him, until he cast a glance towards the elder writer.

Extending a hand towards the approaching guest, Reginald stated, "And there's P. Keith Barnett, a man who's been a huge influence on me."

Stunned, Barnett stopped at the first step leading up to the stage.

Reginald continued, "Mr. Barnett's been so very generous with his advice, and I've learned a lot about professionalism from him, to say nothing of how to sharpen my writing skills. Everything he's told me to do, I've done, and I don't mind letting everyone know how he's become almost like a father to me. Hey, how about a big hand for the guy?"

Barnett reached the podium, his emotions in turmoil. He barely registered Reginald's arm around his shoulder as the room filled with applause. While the clapping died down, the younger man found a chair, leaving Barnett at the podium. He cleared his throat and moved towards the microphone.

"I'm not used to having an opening act," Barnett

quipped. The audience laughed enthusiastically, giving the writer time to take a swig of water and compose himself. "Anyway, thank you, Reginald. And I'd like to thank everyone for taking the time to be here."

"Uh-huh," Reginald said, nodding. "Hey, tell everyone what you keep saying about what's most important about being a professional writer. You know, sacrifice?"

"So much for my lead-in to that idea." Barnett surveyed the audience and smiled softly. "Solid grammar skills, proper pronunciation, and basic story construction are essential to any quality writing, whether it's pulp-style or romance or erotica or the more literary pursuits."

"Oh, yeah," Reginald responded, punching the air. "Or comic books."

"Or comic books," Barnett agreed. "But, I sacrificed –"

"Yeah, this guy gave up television. Can you believe that?" Reginald gave an exaggerated shrug. "I mean a life without cartoons. That's crazy. Who wants to live like that?"

"It's not that horrible, once you realize how much time you waste just keeping the idiot box on for company." Barnett turned to look directly at Reginald. "But being good company is a good step towards being good company for yourself. Thus, you won't need a television filling your head with negativity."

Reginald gulped. "Mm-mm."

Taking a step towards Reginald, Barnett continued, "Also, sacrifice means leaving people behind, psychic vampires who steal your energy and generally mess up your mojo."

The younger man saw the steel in Barnett's eyes and suddenly found himself speechless.

"Being a skilled writer isn't enough. The problem with not being a good neighbor … indeed, a good person … is that it catches up to you and sooner than you hope." Barnett stared at Reginald who blinked nervously.

As soon as beads of nervous perspiration formed on the Reginald's upper lip, Barnett turned to the audience once again. "Anyway, thank you all for being here. I'd like to tell you about my journey and maybe if you want to follow my path to publication, I can give you a little hope."

As Barnett spoke to the audience, Reginald stared at his shoes, silent. He pondered the words directed towards him, his face flushed with embarrassed self-realization.

Several minutes later, Barnett grinned. "Well, you've

listened to me long enough. How about you ask us some questions?" He gestured towards a man in a t-shirt with the image of some anime character and a ring of yellow along the collar created from countless years of sweating and inadequate laundering. "How about you?"

The man stood up, clearly thrilled to be speaking with the author. "You are on the road a lot, according to your website. Where do you go to recharge your mental batteries?"

"Good question," Barnett stated. Predictably, the questioner grinned like he just won the lottery as he sat down to listen. "This is going to sound peculiar, but I live close enough to Midlothian, Illinois that I can frequently visit Bachelors Grove Cemetery. Since I write a lot of horror these days, I go there to seek out my muse among the spirits, demons, and vampires." Barnett smiled as some members of the audience chuckled uncomfortably. "Sorry, did I overshare again?"

Reginald looked up at Barnett and interrupted the relieved laughter. "I only live a couple hours from there."

Barnett nodded, smiled insincerely at Reginald, then addressed the audience once again. "I find the cemetery oddly peaceful, despite its reputation. It's like I hear the spirits of the people who used to picnic there. They tell me their stories, and I become a vessel for their life histories. When I pour out what they give me, I bestow a kind of literary immortality to them. I hope that makes sense."

Most of the audience members smiled and nodded in agreement. Several brought their hands together, clapping.

"As a horror writer, one must look for the beauty in the frightening and the mysterious." Barnett took a deep breath. "I mentioned sacrifice and Bachelors Grove Cemetery is where I make mine." His eyes twinkled as they widened. "Usually this involves a virgin under the full moon. When the spirits whisper to me, that's where I *really* get my story ideas. Besides, what's a human life when it comes to increasing my Amazon Author Ranking?"

As the audience laughed, some a little more nervously than others, and several people rose to give Barnett a standing ovation, Reginald found himself grinding his teeth together.

"And now, would anyone have a question for my young friend?"

Reginald sat up straight in his seat, his shoulders pulled back, and his smile as wide as he could make it, not caring how much it made him look like a comic book villain. He prepared himself for the warmth of the spotlight.

Barnett nodded towards a young woman who wore a onesie designed to resemble a polar bear.

"I really have a question for you, Mr. Barnett," the young woman stated.

Reginald relaxed in his seat, ready to answer the question that would inevitably follow this one. However, for the rest of the hour, no one asked Reginald anything about comics, about publishing, about writing, not even about his ponytail.

For this, I talked Barney up?

Barnett commanded the attention of the eager audience for the remainder of the hour. Reginald didn't appreciate being upstaged one little bit and decided to push his way towards the podium for a reading of his comic reviews. If time permitted, Reginald intended to amaze the audience with his rendition of his favorite rap videos.

Then, Reginald looked up to see the promoter standing at the back of the auditorium. Landry Hills, a slender, middle-aged woman with bright blue hair tied in pigtails, uncrossed her arms and walked towards the stage with purpose. Reginald noticed that her eyes met his frequently and without warmth.

"Ladies and gentlemen," Barnett said, watching Landry approach the stage from the corner of his eye, "this concludes our panel for today. If you have any further questions for Reginald or myself, feel free to visit us at our tables. Thanks for being here and enjoy the rest of the show." By the time the audience concluded their applause, Landry reached the steps and made her way up to the stage.

"Good talk, Keith." Landry shook Barnett's hand warmly. But while the promoter complimented the writer, Reginald moved past them both quickly, then leaped from the top step to the floor.

"Thanks," Keith said with a smile, his gaze following Reginald until the man vanished from sight. "I'm not complaining, mind you, but why did you invite Reginald up here?"

Landry's jaw dropped. "Um, I thought you did." Her eyes narrowed. "I've been getting some … comments about Mr. Kohlman, and I think we need to compare notes."

"I agree." Barnett sighed and realized he'd been clenching his fists.

#

"Hey, Barney!"

As part of the flow of exhibitors leaving the now-ended convention, Barnett flinched when he heard Reginald's voice. He pulled the handcart to a standing position as the younger man sprinted across the auditorium to catch up with him.

Standing beside Barnett, Mary Lou muttered, "So much for a clean escape."

"Have a good show, Barney?" Reginald smiled brightly, his arms extended in preparation to hug either Barnett or Mary Lou, depending on whom responded first.

Barnett placed himself between Mary Lou and her potential assailant. Reginald halted in his tracks when he saw the severity of Barnett's expression. The young writer's cheerful demeanor vanished like frost under the morning sun.

"Listen, Reginald," Barnett stated softly, but with a growl that emanated from the pit of his stomach, "it was very bad form to force your way onto my panel. What possessed you to do that?"

"Jay-*zus*, Barney. I figured you or the promoter made an error in not scheduling me to speak."

"You figured wrong." Barnett cleared his throat. "Reginald, I was young once too. I had a fire in my belly and didn't care much about anyone but myself."

Reginald's smile returned. "Really?"

Barnett bit his lip before replying. "No, not really. I learned courtesy at an early age. My parents taught me about karma and how it can start with simply not being a jerk."

"You mean like you're being now." Reginald smiled as if he'd won an argument that existed only in his head.

"Perhaps," Barnett admitted. "But, my motives are pure, for what that's worth." He sighed. "Young man, you're on a path of professional, and personal, self-destruction. You're rude, you're self-centered, and you're arrogant. You behave as if the convention is all about you being the center of attention and it's not." He paused for effect. "And I've seen how you look at Mary Lou."

Any trace of bemusement fled Reginald's face. "What's your point, Barney?"

"My point," Barnett said earnestly, "is that you don't want to nickel-and-dime your karma into the red zone. Every investment of kindness comes back to you. That's why I mentor young writers to be kind, if nothing else." He grinned. "Actually, I like encouraging people to chase their dreams. The karma is just a bonus." He felt the warmth of Mary Lou's smile and her gentle squeeze of his arm.

Reginald noticed that too and his expression darkened. "So, you're saying you want to take me on as your assistant, maybe teach me to be a writing Jedi like you?"

Barnett's own countenance took a turn towards the grim. "Not at all. I also promote positive behavior from people who want to give to others and leave the writing field better than when they first encountered it. You aren't that person." His tone softened. "I've read your work. It has energy. It has potential, as do you. But why do you think you have to behave like a jerk to be noticed?"

Reflexively, Reginald's face screwed up in confusion and disdain.

"Become a better person, Reginald. You'd be surprised how little it takes and how much of a return you get. And stop calling me 'Barney.'" With that, Barnett spun on his heel to leave. "Good bye, Reginald, and good luck."

Mary Lou nodded towards Reginald as she turned to follow her new mentor.

"See you soon?" Reginald asked the woman, the

hopefulness thick in his voice.

To his disappointment, Mary Lou shook her head and left.

# # #

"Hi, this is Reginald Kohlman, the writer and publisher and creator of Captain Heroic. Ah, you've heard of me? Awesome sauce! Anyway, I'd like to be a guest at your show.

"Oh. Wouldn't you like to know more about me before saying no?

"Oh, you talked to Landry Hills? What did she say?

"Oh. Complaints about poaching customers? Jay-*zus*, I don't even know what that means. Disruptive? Disagreeable? I am not! How many complaints about me? *Really?* Listen, Is P. Keith Barnett going to be there? Good, because you can talk to him and verify that –

"Oh, he already mentioned me too? Good, because I need to sit … oh, he wanted me to sit *where*? That's what Mary Lou Brady said? Hey, I'll have to ask her about that, except she seems to have blocked me on Facebook and Twitter. Anyway, do you want me as a guest, or don't you?

"Oh, you don't? Fine! So, what's your table fee?

"Oh, what do you mean my money doesn't spend?

"Oh … okay. Um … thanks anyway."

# # #

The meatloaf left on the Hello Kitty tray outside Reginald's bedroom achieved room temperature three hours earlier. Reginald's stomach growled loudly in protest from being ignored all day and evening.

The phone screen cast its ghostly illumination over Reginald's tear-streaked face. Barnett hadn't blocked him on social media yet, but he also didn't reply to any of Reginald's "You there?"s.

Reginald ran his hand over his chin thoughtfully. His fingertips scratched the stubble on his face, reminding him that he'd not only missed his meals, his ponytail would be horrendously uneven.

And it was all Barnett's fault. Somehow. *Wasn't it?*

The bedroom door swung open. Edna Kohlman stood framed in the light from the hallway. She held the dinner tray with trembling hands. "Did I do something wrong, honey? I know I didn't consult you about dinner and I'm sorry."

"No," Reginald sighed. "I just had a bad show." He

recalled Mary Lou's expression just before she turned her back to him. "It left me with a bad taste in my mouth." He sighed dramatically. "Mother, do you think I'm a bad person?"

Edna averted her gaze to study her cold meatloaf. "Of course not."

Reginald nodded. "I could have been Barnett's right-hand guy. I could have gotten a leg up in this industry. What do I have to do to reach his level?"

"Maybe if you studied his work," Edna offered. "Learn what inspires him and see if it works for you. Spend extra time on writing more commercial work. Brush up on your grammar."

"Puh-*lease*, Mother! You can freakin' stop now. As for inspiration, Barney ... er, Mr. Barnett claims he sacrifices virgins under the full moon at Bachelors ... he sounds nutty when he says it ... but what if he's not joking?"

Before Reginald could finish his sentence, a new item pushed its way onto the smart phone's glass screen.

P. KEITH BARNETT @ BACHELORS GROVE CEMETERY

A notion rooted in Reginald's imagination and

blossomed immediately. " Bachelors Grove Cemetery?" He snapped his fingers the way he saw numerous actors do on TV when their characters came up with a great idea. "Bachelors Grove Cemetery under the full moon! That's it!"

Reginald's fingers danced over the keyboard of his laptop. A minute later, he cried out "YES!" in a tone worthy of any medical detective show currently on the air. "If I leave now, I might reach Midlothian while it's still sunny."

Edna tried to block the doorway. "But you said this Barney was crazy."

Rising to his feet and thumping his chest dramatically, Reginald announced, "Mother, you have to be crazy to be a writer." A sly grin spread over his features. "And if he's as looney as I believe him to be, I'll catch it on video and send it to the world. So much for the big shot writer." Reginald rubbed his hands together. "Either way, I'll be at his writing level, or he'll be *way* below me. Either way, I rise."

Sliding his feet into his tennis shoes, Reginald Kohlman leaped towards the door, guided Edna from the doorway to the center of the hall, seized the plate with his intended dinner, and kissed his mother on the cheek. Before she could register her son's sudden display of real affection, Reginald slid behind the wheel of the family SUV, keys in hand and prepared to make the trek to Bachelors Grove Cemetery.

# # #

Reginald turned off the car and his GPS in succession once he pulled into his parking space. Only one other car sat in the parking lot across the highway from the entrance to Bachelors Grove.

Why can't they let us park closer? Reginald wondered. *No wonder it's a dump. Maybe if they let people picnic in there again, they might get more business. They could probably even charge admission.* He made a mental note to figure out some kind of marketing plan. *Maybe a spooky theme park thing. Is there room for a roller coaster?*

A figure ran behind Reginald's vehicle, caught for a moment in his rear-view mirror. By the time he released his seat belt, a clearly female shape had already crossed to the far side of Midlothian Turnpike and entered a gap in the greenery that shielded the cemetery from casual view.

Reginald believed the black-clad, slender figure held a bundle under one arm, if that was of any importance. Pulling a small flashlight and his cell phone from his backpack with trembling hands, Reginald took a deep breath, steeling himself for what he was about to do.

The phone caught the 4G signal easily and the BROADCAST NOW button glowed brightly. A touch of the faceplate later, Reginald stared at his own unsmiling countenance in the reflected light of a nearby streetlamp.

"Hi, fans of Captain Heroic," Reginald stated with solemnity. "This is the coolest guy you know, Reginald Kohlman." He replayed his words in his mind. "No, forget that. I've been driving and thinking about my life. I need to become a different person. I can see that now." He paused dramatically. "And, I want you to witness this transformation."

Swallowing hard, Reginald contemplated the results of his impending actions. What if he did become someone different? What if his sacrifice turned out to be his fan base, each and every one of them confused and embarrassed by his actions?

He thumbed the END BROADCAST button on his phone and deleted the video. Reginald promised himself to do a post-event wrap-up, depending on the outcome of his entering the infamous cemetery.

Instead, Reginald elected to activate the video recording app in his phone. *I can always edit this, maybe move into books because that's where the prestige is. Maybe then, Mary Lou will –*

Drawing up short at the thought of her name, Reginald was reminded of his original purpose in driving to this place. He cleared his throat, exited his vehicle, and walked towards the highway.

Fortunately, it was a warm, cloudless night. The full moon shone overhead, almost at the apogee of its path. Reginald slid the phone into his shirt pocket, making sure the lens faced forward.

"I'm going on radio silence now," Reginald whispered to himself as he sprinted across all five lanes of the turnpike and towards the trees that shielded the entrance. Fortunately, the moonlight illuminated the end of the gravel pathway leading towards the cemetery. Soon, Reginald walked stealthily into the tunnel of twisted trees towards the cemetery proper, ignoring the official warning signs forbidding entry after sundown.

Moonlight pierced the holes in the wooden canopy overhead, allowing shafts of silver light to touch the rough pathway below Reginald's feet. He carefully walked around the beams, keeping an eye on the person ahead of him.

To remain as cloaked by the shadows as he could be, he hugged the sides of the path which proved fortuitous because almost halfway down the former road, the slender figure stopped and turned around to see if anyone pursued her.

Reginald's jaw dropped as the figure entered a fragment of moonlight, and he recognized the slender person at last.

Mary Lou Brady looked back towards the entrance intently. Apparently satisfied that she was alone, the woman stopped to remove her shirt, then her jeans, much to Reginald's surprise and elation. Then, she unfurled the bundle she carried, flapping it a couple of times to shake out any wrinkles in the fabric, before pulling it over her head.

Reginald crossed his legs instinctively, his eyes wide to take in the glorious sight before him.

Silver, gold, and scarlet threadwork danced across the robe's purple fabric as it floated in the night breezes, still caressing the young woman's curves. Reginald felt his mouth go dry as he watched Mary Lou gather her street clothing and resume her trek to the cemetery. A few seconds later, Reginald moved down the path to keep pace with her.

Reginald's mind raced. *A robe? If those are symbols stitched into it, I've never seen anything like that in any comic book I've ever read.* His mouth went dry and he wished he'd brought a soda with him. *I thought Barnett was joking about the sacrifice. This is misery.*

Then, Reginald almost stumbled as a random thought entered his mind. *What if she's the sacrifice? What if Barnett intends to kill her because he's nuts, and I might be her only hope. I wonder how grateful she might be ...* With that, Reginald picked up his pace as much as the poor light and the uneven surfaces below his feet would allow.

Soon, Mary Lou emerged into the open area just outside the cemetery gates. With one more glance behind her, she ran through the tornado wire fencing into the heart of the cemetery.

Reginald looked down to see the little red light at the top of his phone still blinking. He allowed himself a smile, knowing he was still recording something for his followers, or perhaps the authorities.

The woman walked towards the Pond where a hooded figure awaited her. The stitching on his own hooded robe, even from a distance, appeared to be more intricate than Mary Lou's own. She said something that Reginald couldn't hear from where he crouched, but by way of reply, the other person pulled back his hood.

If the other figure had been anyone else but P. Keith Barnett, Reginald would have been astonished.

Barnett and Mary Lou embraced, holding each other for several seconds longer than Reginald would have liked to witness. When the two separated, Barnett motioned for Mary Lou to follow him to the center of the burial grounds.

At the edge of the fence surrounding the Pond, Barnett knelt to open a small suitcase, the kind with wheels and retractable handle. From inside, he pulled out a white, rolled-up something-or-other and handed it to Mary Lou. Without another word, she found a level area and unfurled what appeared to be a blanket with a design embroidered on it in black thread. *Okay, this one I recognize.*

A pentagram.

After that, Barnett reached into the valise and withdrew what could only be described as a bad-ass dagger. The steel blade curved like an ocean wave and even from a hundred feet away, Reginald knew that it would probably make a bigger hole coming out than it would going in.

Reginald whispered to his phone, "I guess he wasn't kidding about that sacrifice after all."

"No, he wasn't," Mary Lou called out. "You might as well come on over, Reginald. You suck as a ninja."

"Mm-mm." Reginald stomped over to face Mary Lou,

stopping at the edge of her blanket. He cast his most curious expression at Barnett. The moonlight reflected from the older writer's teeth. Reginald braced himself emotionally for the older man's rebuke.

"Reginald, my boy!" Barnett's grin was as huge and twice as bright as the moon overhead. "Believe it or not, I'm glad you're here." He reached under a fold in his ornately-detailed robe, pulled out a chamois from his pants pocket, then used it to polish the blade thoroughly. "Come over here, why don't you, Reginald?" He strolled towards the far corner of the property.

Almost tripping over the uneven grounds, Reginald jogged to the older man's side.

Barnett waited for Reginald to catch up. The older writer folded his arms, still keeping the dagger in his guest's view. "So why are you here, young man?"

"I want to learn how to do what you do." Reginald steeled his nerve. "I'm down with everything you've told me."

Barnett regarded Reginald through narrowed eyes. "Oh-kay … why *now* would you make the proper sacrifices to gain mastery over your craft?"

"Duh!" Reginald stifled a snort. "I want to get into cons for free. I want to talk before large crowds." Then he took a long look back at Mary Lou. She knelt in the center of the blanket, well within the confines of the pentagram. Framed in the moonlight as she was, Reginald couldn't think of anyone lovelier than this girl at that moment. "And all the other perks that come with fame." Then as an afterthought, "Oh, and I want to be a better person, just like you said."

Reginald's concentration broke when Barnett spoke again. "Hmm … what will you give up? What will you sacrifice to reach your goals?"

Reginald weighed his next words carefully. "Mary Lou is a beautiful woman, more beautiful than anyone I've ever seen." He paused at the precipice of commitment, then threw himself into the abyss. "I would do whatever it took to bring my dreams to life." He glanced at Mary Lou again. "And to impress her. And you."

The smile vanished from Barnett's face. "That's quite a commitment, Reginald."

With that statement, Reginald laughed uproariously. "Jay-*zus*, Barney! You can be my wingman. I think that's pretty good networking, don't you think?"

"Let me tell you about networking, Reginald." Barnett

rested his arm over the younger man's shoulders and led him even further away from where Mary Lou recited some mantra in a language he couldn't identify, each syllable unintelligible from this distance. If she heard Reginald's offer to Barnett, she gave no indication.

"Years ago," Barnett continued, "I was a jerk. I thought I was the next Stan Lee, Alan Moore, or Jerry Siegel. I sold some scripts to some minor comic book companies back during one of the industry's boom periods. This led to other sales from larger outfits and eventually, a full schedule of convention appearances. I thought I was living the rock-and-roll life and I deserved every bit of it." Barnett's gaze dropped towards his hands. "I wasn't a jerk at first. Sorry to say, I proved adept at becoming one."

He sighed with regret. "Obviously, I became too full of myself, too selfish. I tried to steal assignments from other writers, missed the few deadlines I'd been given, and pretty much made an ass of myself at conventions. I was an embarrassment to myself and to my employers who talked to other publishers and editors. I became more trouble than I was worth to the industry and it cut me out like a cancer. A few of my former friends took great pleasure to see my rapid decline."

"But I'm worth it and you know it," Reginald declared. He took a step towards Mary Lou, but Barnett seized him by the shoulder and pulled him back, keeping him by his side.

Ignoring Reginald's statement, Barnett resumed his monolog, "I became industry poison. Fortunately, I ran into a writer at a show who used to be in the field. He sold comics like no one's business before his own fall from grace, just to reappear on all the best seller lists with his novels. He had over a dozen books out at the time that almost refused to go out of print. If I told you his name, I know even you would have heard of him."

"Mm-mm." Reginald turned just as Mary Lou rose to her feet. Her robe hugged her curves almost as much as he desired to, himself. Reginald's fingers moved towards the phone in his shirt pocket, hoping to catch her image for his files later as Barnett guided him back towards the object of his desire.

Ignoring everyone, especially Reginald, Mary Lou lifted her robe, exposing her alabaster flesh and matching underwear while remaining inside the pentagram. As she folded her garment neatly, Reginald felt the earth quaking gently, and his pulse raced for a few seconds until he realized it was Barnett shaking his shoulder, attempting to regain the youth's attention.

"Listen to me, boy," Barnett commanded. "Not everyone gets to learn what I'm sharing with you. For obvious reasons. Imagine the … privilege you are receiving."

"Really?" Reginald grinned, all thoughts of Mary Lou's undress forgotten for the moment. "Oh, statute of limitations. I get it. Go on."

Barnett tucked the chamois back into his pocket. "The other guy took pity on me. He brought me here to this very cemetery and taught me the spells I needed to know, the ones he was given many years before by one of his former editors who also fell on hard times, professionally."

"Sh'yeah," Reginald chuckled.

"I'm not making this up." Barnett circled Reginald until he blocked Reginald's view of Mary Lou's body. "He taught me a spell that allows me to hear the whispers of the deceased. My mentor taught me this incantation and I read the results into a tape recorder. That gave me my first half dozen novels."

"So why are we here?" Reginald swept his arms dramatically, doing a three-sixty to indicate the entire cemetery. "Why not Bachelors Grove Coffee Shop? I mean it might have wi-fi."

"Reginald, this cemetery is a nexus of arcane forces beyond earthly comprehension." Reginald carefully slid the knife into a leather sheath tied to his waist underneath his robe. "This knowledge has been very good to me. The spell can help someone start a new career, someone deserving."

"Which of course," Reginald tapped his chest proudly, "would be me."

Now, it was Barnett's turn to laugh. A heartbeat later, Mary Lou's musical amusement filled the night air as well.

Anger colored Reginald's field of vision. "I know why you have her here, Barney." He paused for drama's sake. "She's your sacrifice."

Mary Lou didn't even bother to hide her grin.

"Laugh it up and forget about being rescued." Reginald turned to a suddenly unamused Barnett. "Listen, I can't say I believe in all this. But what's she got that I don't?"

Barnett gathered his thoughts, his patience nearing its end. "Mary Lou here has a snappy prose style," Barnett stated with an edge in his voice. "She's worked to earn tuition money for college, taking classes when she can afford them. She's worked two jobs at a time and then came home to write."

Realizing how he'd worked himself up, Barnett took a deep, calming breath. "Her mother is in assisted living. Mary Lou wants that dear woman to see her only child making a way in the world before she passes." Barnett waited for the information to sink into Reginald's consciousness. "This young lady just turned twenty-one and Mary Lou's sacrificed more for her dream than any dozen of us would want to." He looked back at her warmly. "She's given up a lot. She's earned her right to be here."

"And what about me?" Reginald tugged at his hair, for once not caring how immaculate it was. "I live in my parents' house, and I'm in my thirties! I've never even been on a date! You think I don't know anything about sacrificing?"

"Compared to whom?" Mary Lou asked coldly. "All you did was let life happen to you."

Reginald jabbed his index finger in Mary Lou's direction. "Listen, I demand to be brought in. Hell, I'll hold you down if Barney's looking for a sacrifice, and *I'm not kidding.*"

Hearing the sincerity in Reginald's fury, Mary Lou and

Barnett exchanged a significant look. Barnett's left eyebrow rose, and Mary Lou nodded. The wind picked up, as if on cue, icy fingers tickling their skins, but paused long enough for Barnett to ask, "And, if I don't?"

Reginald pointed towards the phone in his pocket. "The world learns how cray-cray you really are, Barney. Sorcery and sacrifice, my ass. My vlog audience will love this tale, I'm sure."

"Audience?" Mary Lou grinned.

"Yeah, audience, girl." Reginald savored the feel of his heart pounding and his adrenalin flowing. "Your reps will go straight into the toilet. Now zip it, and I might still let you be my booth babe." Reginald turned towards Barnett again. "Yeah, if I can't be you, Barney, then I'll make sure you can't be you either."

"Way to maintain the karma, Reginald," stated Mary Lou with a mocking smile, refusing to be ignored. "Cray-cray? The stories are real, all of them and then some. The Madonna, the vampires." She grinned. "And the null spots where electronics don't seem to work."

Just as he readied what he believed was a clever remark about the myths surrounding the cemetery, Reginald felt a sharp vibration against his left nipple. He glanced down to his shirt pocket to see the red light on top of his phone fade and completely die.

"No one heard a word of our discussion," Barnett stated. "Mary Lou came up with the plan, in case you wanted a record of this conversation. Clever girl." The older man grinned at his protege.

"The null areas are pretty well mapped out," Mary Lou stated, a rather evil grin spreading across her flawless features. "That's why Keith had you walk through them. All your phone picked up was static until the battery died."

"Suuuure," Reginald said, "Reality doesn't work like that." He glared at Mary Lou. "You didn't know I was tailing you, admit it. You never saw me when you stopped, did you?"

Rolling her eyes, Mary Lou said, "Idiot, I turned around, not because I wanted to make sure I wasn't being followed. I wanted to make certain you *were* following me." She rolled her eyes. "I figured you'd find some way to make your vehicle 'cool.'" Mary Lou provided the air quotes to punctuate her rant. "So, when I saw the Gundam stickers across your back bumper, I knew you'd swallowed our bait."

Hearing the contempt in the voice of perhaps the only woman he felt worthy of being his girlfriend, Reginald felt his arrogance vanishing. His hands shook with mounting fear as he realized how alone he was in this cemetery with a half-naked woman inside a pentagram and a nut with a big, big knife. The phone dropped from his trembling hand onto the grass.

Barnett pulled the knife from under his robes once again. He turned to Mary Lou, indicating Reginald. "No dates, he said?"

"Yep. That's what he said." Her smile betrayed her satisfaction with Reginald's current state of unease. "He practically reeks of chastity."

"S-so?" Reginald swallowed hard. He eyed the exit longingly, but knew that as fast as he thought he could run, that dagger could probably catch him easily. "C'mon," he pleaded, "You've got to admit the recording was pretty clever, and all I get is *this*? Surely I deserve *something* for the drive to Bachelors Grove."

Ignoring Reginald for the moment, Barnett glanced upwards to check the moon's progress through the night sky. With a satisfied nod, Barnett turned to Mary Lou. "It's time."

Mary Lou lifted her eyes towards the moon, now directly shining overhead. She cried out, "I vow to the greater powers below the darkness of the waves that I will use their sorcery and its inspiration wisely." Mary Lou turned towards Barnett and stated solemnly, "Even more importantly, I promise you, Keith, that I will never squander the gift you've given me. I will use my talents for the entertainment of others and to think of others before myself. I do this to balance my karma for the price I am honored to pay." Her eyes lowered. "I am ready to make the agreed-upon sacrifice."

Extending his knife, Barnett watched Mary Lou stretch her right hand towards her mentor in return. He lifted the dagger towards her, the tip of the blade entering the invisible field of protection offered by the pentagram.

"You have been cleansed in the circle of protection," Barnett stated gravely. "Make contact with the bridge between us and thus purified, enter this world once more."

Mary Lou gently gripped the dagger's edge, wrapping her fingers around the sharpened steel. She stepped forward, leaving the pentagram, her blood softly dropping from her hand upon the top of her naked foot.

His terror peaking and his options dwindling, Reginald finally bolted towards the exit from the cemetery. However, with a cobra's speed, Barnett's free hand gripped the younger man's shirt, stopping him in mid-step. For a moment,

Reginald contemplated putting on a burst of speed, but this was his favorite shirt and he didn't want to rip it.

Turning around, Reginald's horror intensified as he realized Barnett didn't even look at him.

Reginald's eyes locked with Mary Lou's. Now, out of the pentagram, she released the dagger and smiled warmly at Barnett who now opened his hand, exposing the handle of the dagger to the night.

Mary Lou's bloodied fingers seized the leather-covered handle of Barnett's knife. She lifted it slowly over her head, admiring its heft and balance. Then, she turned towards Reginald, her eyes glowing with anticipation.

Barnett pulled Reginald close enough to put his forearm around his captive's throat. "Reginald, you wanted to be the center of attention? Now's the moment you've waited for."

The younger man clawed desperately at his would-be mentor's arm as he croaked, "My parents will miss me. I've seen enough TV shows to know CSI will find me."

Barnett smiled as he looked back at the Pond. "Oh, I'm not worried about anyone finding you, Reggie. I'll just stick you underwater with the others." He chuckled. "Never dated, you say. Never had a girlfriend?"

As Mary Lou came closer, the knife now raised high above her head, Reginald Kohlman went limp in Barnett's arms. "No ... never," he admitted.

"No real surprise." Although Reginald couldn't see it, Barnett appeared to be sad. "Are you prepared, Mary Lou? Have you said your dark prayers to our ocean-bound benefactors? Are you ready to complete the ritual?"

"I am. I have, my teacher." Mary Lou's eyes met Reginald's for the last time. "You know, I saw how you looked at me, like I was some kind of meat trophy, the same as every man did, except one." She smiled softly at Barnett. "You know, I meant it when I told Keith that I'd kill to be as good a writer as he is ... and to be able to help other authors achieve their dreams."

Reginald turned his head to meet Barnett's gaze. "I could have taught you too, young man. But when you threw Mary Lou under the bus ..." With a frown, he added, "Karma doesn't always wait to settle accounts."

"You're crazy!" Reginald cried.

"You have to be," Barnett declared, "to be a writer."

With that, Mary Lou Brady brought the dagger down in a swift, smooth motion, lodging it in the center of Reginald's heart. Immediately, Reginald felt his soul leave his body, or perhaps his own imagination kicked in just before the moment of his death.

He looked down to see Mary Lou's eyes go wide with wonder. Barnett smiled at her, and she nodded vigorously. The older man reached into the depths of his robes and pulled out a digital tape recorder.

Mary Lou snatched the device from his hand and thumbed it to life. She spoke at a madman's pace, thoughts and stories and plotlines spilling from the depths of the innermost corners of her imagination. Reginald marveled at the ingenuity of her stories ... stories that could have been his.

The woman laughed as she shouted, "One at a time. One at a time. I hear you all."

At that moment, Reginald felt his eternal essence floating above his body, and the last voice he heard in this life was the man he now wished he could have been in so many ways.

"Behold the rarest, and most effective, type of sacrifice there is," P. Keith Barnett explained to his new assistant. "*Virgin* sacrifice."

# # #

"The Rawhide City Comic Convention is honored to present its guest of honor, *New York Times* best-selling author, Mary Lou Brady!" For a few seconds, applause drowned out the inevitable feedback that wailed from the public address system. "She's got fresh copies of *The Virgin Dies at Midnight* at her table and she'd love to talk to you."

"So, you wrote a big-selling book, huh?" Mal Taronan reluctantly moved his attention from the front of Mary Lou's blouse to the back cover of her novel. "That's kinda crazy, babe."

At the next table, P. Keith Barnett handed a plastic bag filled with his books to another satisfied customer, along with her credit card. He thanked the woman and turned his smile towards Mary Lou. He arched his eyebrow.

By way of silent reply, Mary Lou slowly drew a long, black fingernail across her soft throat as she nodded at her mentor. She then gently pulled her book from Mal's sweaty grasp.

With an unblinking, wide-eyed stare that made Mal's breath catch in his throat, she asked, "Haven't you heard? You've got to be crazy to be a writer."

Final Thoughts

The last couple of years have been quite the adventure.

Of course, Charles and I continue to plan future issues of *The Haunting Tales of Bachelors Grove*. Current plans call for eighteen issues, released in spans of six, as well as solo comics with some of our real-life celebrities that inhabit the Midlothian Universe, a couple of annuals, solo comics featuring Ron Fitzgerald and other special guest stars, along with at least one Holiday Special.

We also plan to work on other comics including a superhero title as well as an outreach tool for police departments across the country.

Meanwhile, Charles partners with companies to publish special interest comics as he puts together more work under the Silver Phoenix Entertainment banner.

And I continue to write not only for Silver Phoenix Entertainment, but for my own Rising Tide imprint, as well as for other publishers.

Would I have considered writing horror before now? Probably not, but now that I've tapped into the dark side of my psyche, I believe the only limitations I have are the ones I impose on myself.

In addition to being entertained, I sincerely hope you

learn something from my journey, that despite my advancing years, the voyage has merely begun.

May you stretch, may you grow, may you discover more aspects to yourself worth celebrating.

And never be caught in Bachelors Grove Cemetery after dark.

References

We've mentioned a lot of cool people in the pages of this book. If you wish to know more about some of them, here are their websites:

KADROLSHA ONA CAROLE is a healer, psychic, television personality, actress, entrepreneur, and real-life super-heroine. She's the Queen of the Paranormal and she's the real deal. Find out more about this amazing woman at www.queenoftheparanormal.com or her Facebook page.

RON FITZGERALD is not just the Master of dark, sticky Goth illusion, he's also an actor and one of the coolest guys you could ever hope to meet. Check out his history and future projects at www.fitzgeraldsrealm.com or you can visit his Facebook page.

SILVER PHOENIX ENTERTAINMENT is the Midwest's largest producer of horror, public service, and Roller Derby comics. For more information about their creators and current projects, as well as the Writers Guidelines for *The Haunting Tales of Bachelors Grove*, go to silverphoenix.net as well as their Facebook page.

BRIAN K. MORRIS, Silver Phoenix's Editor-in-Chief, writes for numerous independent comic book and prose publishers. He lives in Central Indiana with his wife, no children, no pets, and too many comic books. His weekly writing blog, "Novel Writing Made Less Impossible" appears at www.freelance-words.com. He also has Facebook pages for his Rising Tide publishing imprint, as well as a page dedicated to Vulcana.

TREVOR ERICK HAWKINS' artwork appears in many private collections as well as the Gone With the Wind Museum in Marietta, Georgia. He's participated in Fine Art showings in Georgia, Tennessee, and Illinois. In addition to being the Art Director for Rising Tide Publications, his paintings have appeared on the covers for *Santastein: The Post-Holiday Prometheu*s and *Vulcana: Rebirth of the Champion*, the latter of which he co-created with author Brian K. Morris. Trevor is available for personal appearances and special commissions. He can be contacted at www.popimages4U.com.

OTHER WORKS
BY
BRIAN K. MORRIS

From **Kindle Worlds**

Bloodshot: The Coldest Warrior

From **Freelance Words**

Santastein: The Post-Holiday Prometheus
(with cover by TREVOR ERICK HAWKINS

Conflict: A Study In Heroic Contrasts

Vulcana: Rebirth of the Champion
(with cover by TREVOR ERICK HAWKINS)

From **Rising Tide/ACE Comics Publications**

The Original Skyman Battles the Master of Steam (with an introduction by ROY THOMAS and cover by PAT BOYETTE)

To purchase Brian's work, go to

www.amazon.com/author/briankmorris

**All selections are available in either
e-book or paperback formats**
(except *Bloodshot: The Coldest Warrior*
which is in e-book form only)

Anthology Appearances

With Great Power
(Edited by Rick Phillips, Dinky Productions)
Malicious Mysteries
(Edited by Jeffrey Allan Davis, GCD Publishing)
Metahumans Vs. the Ultimate Evil
(Edited by J.L. McDonald and Jim Robb, Lion's Share Press)
Quest for the Space Gods: The Chronicles of Conrad von Honig
(Edited by Jim Beard & John C. Bruening, Quirk Press)

"*A Rising Tide Lifts All Boats.*"

YOU'VE READ
THE BOOK ...

SILVERPHOENIX.NET